"So how come you didn't remarry?" Dev asked.

"I just like my life as it is. I'm content, aren't you? We both ended up with what we wanted, or we'd be leading totally different lives right now." Beth was embarrassed and babbling, and couldn't seem to stop.

At his continued silence, she ventured a quick glance at him. At least he wasn't laughing…

Dev stared down at her, his eyes intent and searching her own. "I really enjoyed walking with you. Maybe another time?"

"I'd like that."

He strolled away and Beth continued on to her store, reining in the urge to look back.

Just a walk. A casual conversation. Nothing more. Yet she could still feel the tingle in the hand he'd held, still felt that little sense of loss when he'd released it.

There was no use denying it. Their old chemistry was still there, and it intensified every time she ran into him….

Books by Roxanne Rustand

Love Inspired

*Winter Reunion

*Aspen Creek Crossroads

Love Inspired Suspense

**Hard Evidence	†Final Exposure
**Vendetta	†Fatal Burn
**Wildfire	†End Game
Deadly Competition	
	**Snow Canyon Ranch
	†Big Sky Secrets

ROXANNE RUSTAND

Roxanne Rustand lives in the country with her husband and a menagerie of pets, many of whom find their way into her books. She works part-time as a registered dietitian at a psychiatric facility, but otherwise you'll find her writing at home in her jammies, surrounded by three dogs begging for treats, or out in the barn with the horses. Her favorite time of all is when her kids are home— though all three are now busy with college and jobs.

This is her twenty-fourth novel, and the first in her Aspen Creek Crossroads series for Love Inspired. Her next book will be *Murder at Granite Falls* for Love Inspired Suspense, April 2011. *RT Book Reviews* nominated her for a Career Achievement Award in 2005, and she won the magazine's award for Best Superromance of 2006.

She loves to hear from readers! Her snail-mail address is P.O. Box 2550, Cedar Rapids, Iowa 52406-2550. You can also contact her at www.roxannerustand.com, at www.shoutlife.com/roxannerustand, or through her blog, where readers and writers talk about their pets, at roxannerustand.blogspot.com.

Winter Reunion
Roxanne Rustand

Steeple
Hill®

Published by Steeple Hill Books™

STEEPLE HILL BOOKS

Steeple
Hill®

Recycling programs
for this product may
not exist in your area.

ISBN-13: 978-0-373-87633-4

WINTER REUNION

Copyright © 2010 by Roxanne Rustand

All rights reserved. Except for use in any review, the reproduction
or utilization of this work in whole or in part in any form by any
electronic, mechanical or other means, now known or hereafter
invented, including xerography, photocopying and recording, or in
any information storage or retrieval system, is forbidden without
the written permission of the editorial office, Steeple Hill Books,
233 Broadway, New York, NY 10279 U.S.A.

This is a work of fiction. Names, characters, places and incidents are
either the product of the author's imagination or are used fictitiously, and
any resemblance to actual persons, living or dead, business establishments,
events or locales is entirely coincidental.

This edition published by arrangement with Steeple Hill Books.

® and TM are trademarks of Steeple Hill Books, used under license.
Trademarks indicated with ® are registered in the United States Patent
and Trademark Office, the Canadian Trade Marks Office and in other
countries.

www.SteepleHill.com

Printed in U.S.A.

This is what the Lord says: "Stand at the crossroads and look; ask for the ancient paths, ask where the good way is, and walk in it, and you will find rest for your soul."

—*Jeremiah* 6:16

With love to my mother, Arline, whose strength, Swedish determination and whimsical sense of humor has always been my greatest inspiration. She always encouraged me to follow my dreams, and even when I was a little girl, she thought I should be a writer someday. So Mom, this one is for you!

Chapter One

Beth Carrigan took a last glance at her cell phone, shoved it into her pocket and heaved a sigh.

A crisp, sunny October weekend in Aspen Creek, Wisconsin, usually brought crowds of tourists from Chicago, Minneapolis, and all parts in between.

It didn't bring unexpected calls from Washington, D.C., California, and the Henderson Law Office. Calls that now had her stomach doing crazy cartwheels.

What on earth was she going to do?

But everything is going to be fine, Lord. It's going to be fine, right? She surveyed her bookstore, breathing in the beloved scents of books, dark-roast coffee and apricot tea as she walked to the back, where her friends were already settled in an eclectic mix of comfy upholstered chairs and rockers.

Their voices fell silent as three pairs of worried eyes looked up at her. Their concern was so palpable that she forced herself to dredge up a nonchalant smile. "How's the coffee? Is it better this time? I bought a new fair trade brand and—"

"The question is, how are *you?*" Olivia Lawson, the oldest book-club member at fifty-six, had been an adjunct professor of literature at an exclusive private college in Chicago before walking away from the rat race and moving to Aspen Creek to teach at the community college.

Her eyebrows, dark in contrast to her short, prematurely silver hair, drew together in a worried frown. "You definitely look upset. Did that fool banker deny your loan application again?"

"No news." Beth closed her eyes briefly for a quick silent prayer over the vacant building next door, where she hoped to open a gift shop and provide space for a youth center on the upper level.

Keeley North, owner of an antiques shop a few blocks away, snorted. "If it's those vandals again, we can all march over to the sheriff's office and make sure he takes things seriously this time."

Despite her worries, Beth smiled. Blond, blue-eyed, with an effervescent sense of humor that belied her bulldog tenacity, Keeley was loyal to a fault. Beth could easily see her backing the sheriff into a corner until he called in the National Guard. "No vandals. It's…well, a little more complicated than that."

"If this is a bad time, we can all leave, dear." Olivia frowned. "Unless, of course, there's something we can do to help."

For years, they'd been meeting twice a month on Saturday mornings, an hour before the store opened.

The five members had been friends in good times and bad, and though Hannah was away to help with family problems in Texas, Beth knew she could count on every one of them for support and the utmost discretion. Still, she stumbled over her thoughts trying to frame her news in the best light.

"The first call was from my mother. She's taking the scenic route from California, and will arrive here next weekend. For *two whole weeks*."

"How wonderful." The glint in her eyes betrayed Olivia's true feelings. "You two can spend some quality time together, and catch up."

Beth bit her lower lip. "I hope so…if things go better this time. Usually she comes wanting to revamp my whole life, but she didn't sound quite that upbeat on the phone. I hope everything is all right."

Sophie Alexander, the youngest of the group at twenty-nine, slowly shook her cap of short auburn hair. "Last time you were frazzled for months afterward, just trying to find everything."

"Believe me, if Mom just spends every minute rearranging my house and the store again, I'll be very thankful." Beth took a deep breath. "Because that second call was from Dev. He's coming back on Monday, and plans to be in town for a week."

Olivia's mouth dropped open. "Your mother and ex-husband. In the same town." She paused for a moment, then tilted her head and angled a speculative look at Beth. "And he called you to say he's coming. Interesting."

"Believe me, there's no love lost between us now. When he filed for divorce, it was *final*." Beth winced, trying to hold back the painful memories of the day he'd announced that he wanted to end their marriage… and the even more painful memories of what happened later. "I haven't heard a word from him since, other than when he came back to town for his mother's funeral six months ago."

"As I remember, it wasn't exactly a friendly meeting." Keeley frowned. "I know it was a funeral and all, but he barely *acknowledged* you."

And Beth had had trouble controlling her hurt and anger even during that brief encounter, though she'd known it was her duty to attend. "Well, he won't be in town long this time either, before he heads right back to the Middle East…or wherever it is he's stationed. That was the drill throughout our marriage, and I'm sure he hasn't changed."

Sophie shuddered. "This should be interesting."

"I don't even know why he bothered to let me know he's coming." Beth managed an offhand smile. "But it's a blessing to know in advance. With luck, I can make sure my mom and I don't run into him, and all will be well. I doubt he'll be out and about much."

A hush fell over the group. "Is—is he all right?" Keeley ventured after an awkward pause.

"He mentioned a shoulder injury—enough to land him at Walter Reed for a few weeks. He's on medical leave right now."

"When I provide physical therapy for a rotator cuff I tell my patients it'll take a good six months to heal, and for some it's almost a year. A contaminated battle wound could be much worse." Sophie's brow furrowed. "Will he end up with a medical discharge?"

"I asked, but he vehemently denied it." She felt a twinge in a small, scarred part of her heart as she recalled just how dedicated Dev was to military service. Nothing had mattered more to him. Not his family, not her. "He…sounded awfully touchy when I asked."

There'd been a time when she would've given anything for him to come home for good. But those romantic feelings were long gone, and now she felt only sympathy for a man whose entire adult life had been focused on covert operations that he could never discuss. If he had to leave the service, she could only imagine how difficult the adjustment would be.

Olivia shook her head. "That has to be tough."

"Definitely, but he'll have a lot of options once he takes possession of his inheritance. His parents bought up a lot of cheap property long before the town became such a tourist destination. They owned this whole block, and I can't imagine what it's all worth now." Beth hesitated. "That third phone call a few minutes ago was from the family's attorney."

"The attorney called *you?*" Sophie's soft green eyes filled with worry. "That doesn't sound good."

"I'm supposed to be there for the reading of Vivian's will. It's just a formality, though. Dev is the only heir."

"Wow. It sure took a long time to settle things."

"Apparently Vivian was very specific about wanting both of us present, even if it meant a long delay because of his military service."

Just the thought of that meeting gave her jitters.

Dev had betrayed their relationship. Thrown away her love, and left her to face the worst experience of her life alone. She'd prayed hard, trying to forgive him, and maybe she had, but seeing him again would reopen those wounds.

And worse, Dev had made it plain during their divorce that he'd never live in Aspen Creek again. Would he callously decide to terminate her lease so he could sell all of his parents' property to the highest bidder?

If he did, she'd lose her home and her livelihood. Her customers and the members of the book club were like family to her, and she'd lose them as well, if she couldn't find another affordable location in this town.

And the bitter end of their marriage made it all a distinct possibility.

Keeley sat forward in her chair and shoved a strand of gleaming, honey-blond hair behind her ear. "Now, that's intriguing. You need to be there for the reading of the will, but you've been divorced, what—a year?"

"About that." Thirteen months and two weeks, to be exact, though she'd never admit to being so aware of the time frame.

"Maybe she left everything to you."

"And not to their only child? No way."

Keeley's irreverent grin matched the sparkle in her eyes. "All the more reason to at least divide it up."

"A will might have been drawn up during the years Dev and I were still married, but I'm sure his mother wasted no time amending it. She always thought he'd married down the social scale and way too young, even though he was twenty-one. And honestly," Beth added with a rueful laugh, "she was probably right on both counts."

"He was lucky to find someone like you," Sophie said staunchly.

"My own mother wasn't much happier, believe me." Beth shrugged. "I'll show up at that meeting, then slip away so Dev and the lawyer can get down to business. If I can just get past this next week, then everything should go back to normal. I hope."

Dev wearily dropped his duffel bag at his feet, fished a key out of his pocket and opened the front door of the empty Walker building to look inside. The massive limestone walls of the two-story structure had stood solid and uncompromising for over a hundred years, home to everything from a turn-of-the-century wood mill to a medical office and finally the law offices of a long-departed attorney and his partners back in the 1980s.

It was at one end of the block-long row of four large buildings his parents had owned, which all backed up to Aspen Creek. The middle two buildings had been leased as storage for the past few years, though one of them was now empty. The bookstore was the only busy commercial establishment at this end of Hawthorne Avenue.

At that thought, he sighed.

After the reading of his mother's will, he'd need to make some hard decisions about the family home and all of this property, and he'd need to do it fast, before he shipped out to the Middle East again. But what would happen to Beth's beloved store if he sold out? He knew she couldn't possibly have the money to buy it.

He took a step into the empty building and surveyed the trash, old lumber and crumbling boxes that had accumulated inside over the years.

During some of his long, cold and deathly quiet nights on recon missions since his mother's death, he'd sometimes let his mind wander back to this building, and to what he'd do with it. Since it had been vacant for a few years, would it even attract buyers?

Yet the old building seemed like a perfect location for a fine restaurant, or an upscale clothing store of some kind. Or even better, a high-adventure sporting-goods store, with kayak and canoe rentals handled at the walk-out basement level, where customers would be able to launch practically from the back door. Surely the increasing tourism in the area could draw buyers with something like that in mind.

He stifled a flash of regret at imagining the place belonging to someone else. He certainly wasn't planning to stay in town, much less start a business, and sentiment wouldn't pay the real estate taxes at the end of the year, or the cost of ongoing upkeep, either.

Selling it to the right buyers would even bring more traffic to this secluded street and help Beth's bookstore in the process, which would all be for the good.

Beth.

Running a hand over the rough stone walls, he tried to force her from his thoughts, but her image stayed there—wounded, vulnerable, betrayed—with the shock and pain still in her eyes at the moment he'd demanded a divorce and then walked out of her life.

Maybe he could finally absolve some of his own guilt if he were to set a rock-bottom price and a no-interest payment contract, to ensure that she could buy her beloved building. He owed her that and more, for how badly he'd treated her.

If she was even willing to talk to him about it. He certainly had no doubts about what her reaction would be when they met face-to-face at the lawyer's office.

Her formal, distant words and cool nod of sympathy at his mother's funeral marked a chasm between them that had probably only deepened since then.

He'd be lucky if she even showed up. But what did he expect, after what he'd done to her? She'd been a forever kind of woman and she'd deserved so much more than someone as damaged as him.

At the oddly magnified sound of approaching footsteps, he lifted a hand to adjust his new hearing aid and froze, his senses still hyperalert as he fought a flashback to mortar fire and an explosion of rock and steel. For a split second he couldn't draw breath in the choking dust of it all. Felt the searing pain. Saw the crumpled bodies—all that was left of his squad.

His buddies for the past ten years, and the only family he knew beyond the parents who'd estranged themselves from him so long ago.

That he'd been the one left with just wounds and a severe, temporary hearing loss filled him with renewed guilt and sorrow every single day.

He forced himself to relax and look over his shoulder,

and found Nora Henderson sauntering toward him with a briefcase in one hand and a stack of manila folders held in the crook of her other arm.

She nodded toward the law office across the street. "Mondays are usually quiet, and I finished with my previous appointment a little early. If you're ready, come on over."

"And Beth?" The name felt soft and sweet, like the woman herself, and he found himself reining in emotions he'd thought long dead.

The attorney shifted her load and snagged a cell phone from her briefcase. "We definitely need her, too. I'll give her a call."

"Can I ask why she has to be there? I thought everything was settled during our divorce."

A flicker of a smile touched the older woman's lips as she veered off to cross the street. "I'm simply following your mother's instructions," she said over her shoulder. "She was always remarkably specific, you know. See you in a few minutes?"

Memories swamped him as he watched the lawyer walk away. *Remarkably specific.* Now that was hitting the nail square on the head for *both* of his parents, he thought with a hollow, silent laugh.

They'd planned every step of his education. Every decision had been theirs, without fail, no matter what he'd wanted, right down to where he would go to college for premed, the GPA he had to earn, and which medical school he would attend.

They'd brooked no arguments. Hadn't listened. Within their social circle, they'd been lauded as model parents. But when he'd run off to join the military, it had been as much an escape as it was a career choice.

And his father had never spoken to him again.

Beth felt a prickle of uneasiness skitter down her spine when the legal secretary gave her a knowing smile and waved her back to Nora's office.

Her uneasiness exploded into full-fledged anxiety when she arrived to find Dev already seated, his broad shoulders dwarfing one of the two leather chairs facing Nora's desk. Clenching her jaw, she wished she could be anywhere else.

She'd expected gaunt, hospital pallor, and had prepared to offer cool, detached sympathy. She hadn't expected this. His overlong, midnight hair was past due for a cut. The five-o'clock shadow roughening his jaw and black polo shirt stretched over heavily muscled biceps gave him a dark and dangerous air.

Which, she supposed, was warranted, given what he did for a living, though it seemed out of place in this genteel little tourist town.

He moved to rise at her appearance but she waved him down into his chair as she sat and tried for a nonchalant air. "Nora, Dev. Nice to see you both, but I'm not sure why I need to be here."

Dev's intent gaze swept over her, then turned back to Nora. "A formality?"

Nora lifted a folder from the stack on her desk and opened it. "More than that," she murmured. "Vivian and Alan were wonderful people. They cared deeply about their church, their community and their son. They wanted to make changes in their world while they were alive, and wanted it to continue after their deaths."

Clearly uncomfortable at her words, Dev hitched a shoulder. "If they left everything to the church, I'm cool with that. I'm not sticking around in this town at any rate."

"Not all families are quite so understanding, believe me. This office can turn into a war zone at the drop of a hat." Nora smiled at him. "But while your parents did leave some of their liquid assets as a bequest for the church, that wasn't the major part of their estate."

The attorney sifted through the papers in front of her and began reading a long document detailing a number of other bequests to local charities, shirttail relatives and to several close friends.

Beth shifted in her seat and shot a surreptitious look at Dev. His casual demeanor revealed little concern about the proceedings…though as the only heir, he certainly didn't need to worry. His father had been a popular small-town doctor, and his mother had come from an old-money family out East.

Whether or not he returned to active military service, his future would be secure.

Well, good for him. The sooner he left town, the sooner the painful knot in her stomach would ease.

Dev jerked upright at the same moment Beth heard her own name. She tuned back in to the lawyer's words.

Dev shot a glance at Beth, then turned back to the lawyer. "You're kidding."

"I'm afraid not, Dev."

Confused, Beth looked between the two of them. "What?"

"Vivian made these…adjustments to her will after her husband's death." Nora tapped the paper in front of her. "She said Alan might not have approved, but she had good reasons, and as a woman of sound mind, she had the right to make any changes she wished. Are you familiar with the family home, Beth?"

"Well, yes. Of course. I haven't been there for many years. After Alan died, Vivian moved to a condo and turned their home into Sloane House—a boardinghouse."

"Not just any boarders. She took in people who had faced troubles and needed encouragement, a safe haven or a little boost in life. She helped them get on their feet."

"How?"

"Some just needed an affordable place to stay so they could save money toward a rent deposit or down payment on a place of their own. Some had been downsized or out of the workforce for years, so she helped them look for jobs and prepare for interviews, or find loans for reeducation. Some needed help connecting with the right kinds of county services."

"My mother, the social worker," Dev said drily. "That isn't how I remember her while I was growing up."

Nora looked at him over the rims of her glasses. "You've been gone many years. People change."

"I guess, but she sure never said anything about this in her Christmas letters."

"She did know her limitations. She didn't have a

degree in social work, just a big heart. She considered this her ministry, and it meant the world to her when members of her flock succeeded."

"She was certainly discreet," Beth murmured. "I just knew there were boarders living there."

"Which is exactly what she wanted the town to know, for the privacy of those who received her help."

"Still, I'm not sure what this has to do with me."

Nora smiled. "Vivian was worried about the future of any boarders who might be living there after she died."

"So my mother decided we ought to be partners, in the business sense," Dev added, giving Beth a sharp look. "She added a clause to her will requiring that we operate her boardinghouse. Together. For a minimum of six months."

The heat of Dev's stare scorched her skin, and Beth suddenly felt faint. "*Both of us?* Why?"

Nora pursed her lips. "I suspect Vivian thought Devlin would need help, but it's probably a little more complicated than that."

"Well, it won't work. Period. I was due to re-up last month, but had to postpone it until my next checkup at a VA hospital." Dev sat back in his chair, his spine rigid. "I've already made an appointment in Minneapolis on the fifteenth. Once I'm cleared, I'll go active as soon as I can arrange the flights."

"You would need to extend your leave, of course."

He stared at her for a long moment. "That's…that's not possible."

"After all your years in the service, these circum-

stances surrounding your mother's estate, and the fact
that you are due to re-up, I'd bet it's very possible," Nora
mused, giving him a thoughtful look. "If you wanted to
try."

"I have no experience with the care of the elderly, at
any rate."

"These people aren't just old folks, believe me. Beth
leased her bookstore and the apartment above it from
your parents. Correct?"

He gave a single terse nod.

"Do you remember Vivian saying she wanted to give
you one of the buildings when you retired from active
service? She always hoped you'd come back home and
start some sort of business here."

"That was years and years ago, right after I enlisted,"
Dev said, his voice touched with regret. "I guess emo-
tions were running pretty high at the time. I told her that
I would never move back under any circumstances."

"Mothers can have amazing memories where their
children are concerned." Nora canted her head as she
looked between the two of them. "That block is part of
the estate, as you know. But if the terms of the will aren't
met, all of the commercial property will go to Dev's
uncle, Stan Murdock, and their home will be given to
a women's shelter. Dev would only inherit his parents'
personal possessions."

Dev drew in a sharp breath. "Stan is aware of
this?"

"Definitely. He…ah…has voiced considerable interest in razing the entire block for condo development."

Nora arched an eyebrow. "He's actually starting to make plans, as he's quite sure you'll decide to walk away."

Which meant that all the beautiful old stone buildings—including her beloved bookstore and her pretty little apartment above—would fall to a wrecking ball. Her heart sinking, Beth stared at Nora, then she twisted in her chair to face Dev. "Are you going to let him do that?" she whispered.

"He can't." A muscle ticked at the side of his jaw. "That block was designated for preservation as a historic site. My parents worked on the application years ago."

"True. But apparently there were errors in the paperwork filed by the county attorney, and Stan found some loopholes." Nora's mouth curled with disgust. "And with his political connections, he must figure he'll have no trouble doing what he wants. He had an architect come with him from St. Paul earlier this week. The two of them walked the area so preliminary drawings could be made. They stopped in here to discuss how soon Stan could take possession, as if it were a done deal."

Beth sat back in her chair, appalled. "So your uncle would destroy part of the historic section of this town just to make money."

"He's not a blood relative of mine." Dev's expression darkened. "He was my late aunt's second husband. He's a successful businessman in the Twin Cities area and a big donor at charity events. But even as a kid I heard him talk about wheeling and dealing to get exactly what he wanted. I still can't believe Mom would even *consider* letting him get his hands on her property. Is there any way around it?"

"You mean, if Beth alone complied with the will, or the two of you hired a manager to take over the board-inghouse? No. Vivian made sure of it."

"I could retain another lawyer to challenge the will."

"You're welcome to do so. In fact, I'd encourage it, just so you'll feel you've had your best shot at this." Nora shrugged. "But I've represented your family's interests for over twenty years, so please do understand that my concern is for Vivian's wishes along with the well-being of every family member—you included. If I thought there was a way around the stipulations in your mother's will, I'd let you know. But," she added with a faint smile, "I was the one who wrote it up, and I made *sure* it was ironclad, at her express instructions. Unless, of course, you'd returned from the military too disabled to function as an independent adult."

Beth clutched the arms of her chair. "So if Dev and I manage the boardinghouse, he can receive his full inheritance and protect the property. What does this entail, exactly?"

"It certainly isn't a full-time job for those six months. Vivian figured twenty hours a week, more or less, shared between the two of you. You'll manage the house and grounds—maintenance and so on."

"'And so on' could cover a lot of things."

"You'd be expected to provide assistance and encour-agement for the remaining residents, if they need or request it. That might entail helping with searches for jobs, or locating opportunities for school or training. Help with transportation, if need be. Vivian wanted her last boarders to be assisted in every way toward independence, so they can move on to careers or a happy life elsewhere. It's what she would've done for them if she hadn't passed away."

"And if they don't...succeed?"

"Then the estate is tied up for a final six-month period to give you more time. If it's deemed that you made little effort to assist the boarders, then the property goes to Stan. And, of course, the boardinghouse would be closed and any remaining boarders would have to leave."

Dev frowned. "What about day-to-day management of the house itself?"

"The residents each make their own breakfast and lunch, but take turns cooking supper for the group. Vivian worked with them as needed on the planning, budgeting and shopping lists."

"And she left a list of reliable repair people, right?"

"Viv was actually quite handy, though she had to hire repairmen now and then."

"My *mother?*"

A grin briefly touched Nora's lips. "She certainly evolved, over time. She told me that a service manual or a quick search on Google usually provided all she needed to know."

"And the lawn?"

"A lawn-care service could take care of the grass and snow removal, but the monthly budget is limited to the amount of rent paid plus a small stipend. So if you choose to take care of things yourself, it would save money for the bigger problems."

Beth thought for a moment, trying to remember

the old folks she'd seen toddling around town. "What if a resident is simply unable to reach independence? And who judges whether everything has been accomplished—or can't be?"

"This isn't an assisted-living situation. All of the residents are capable of independence and are of reasonable working age, as that was a stipulation before they could move in." Nora folded her hands over the file on her desk. "As far as monitoring the success of the operation goes, a lawyer from Madison and I have been left with that responsibility. Our assignment is to put the welfare of the residents above everything else, and that's what we will do."

"What does that mean, exactly?"

Nora smiled. "You and Devlin will be running the show completely. Harold Billingsly and I will be reviewing the financial summary you two submit each month, along with an update on each resident."

"Update?"

"A written report. Obviously, these people can't be just booted out and set adrift—there needs to be a concrete plan and a move to *successful* independence."

Beth felt the noose tightening.

It all sounded simple. Straightforward. But could she handle working with Dev on a daily basis? Even now, she felt the ragged edges of her emotions unraveling.

Yet if she didn't cooperate, Dev would lose the property, and when Stan took over, she'd lose her home and her store. And those poor folks might end up out on the street. *Lord, tell me what to do here.*

Realizing the room had gone silent, Beth shook off

her thoughts. "I'll try. But I have a bookstore to run, with just one part-time employee who'll soon be going on maternity leave, and I easily put in fifty hours there myself. I'm just not sure I can take on a lot more."

"You're *debating* about this?" Dev's voice turned bitter.

At his tone, she stared back at him in disbelief. He really had no idea. "I said I'll try. It isn't going to be easy."

"But we both have to cooperate, because my dear mother set quite a trap." He made an impatient sound deep in his throat. "If either of us walks away from this, everyone loses. But if we can put up with each other for six months, then everyone wins. Including you."

"*Put up* with each other?" His sharp words stung, reawakening the pain and devastating disillusionment she'd experienced over their divorce, and reminding her of all the reasons she'd hoped to never run into him again.

"Look, I know that working together is the last thing either of us wants. But didn't you hear what Nora said? Cooperate and you'll own your building, free and clear. Even if you despise me, isn't that reward enough?"

Chapter Two

"I—I don't know what you're talking about." Beth stared at Dev in shock, wishing she hadn't let her thoughts wander earlier. "We're divorced. I shouldn't inherit anything."

"Apparently my mother thought otherwise." He shrugged. "Maybe it's like Nora said—she didn't trust me to handle this on my own. So giving you a chance to own your building was a way to ensure your cooperation."

"It wasn't a trust issue," Nora interjected. "I can promise you that. She probably just felt that your current...job skills weren't attuned to this kind of role."

"But the *building*," Beth insisted. "That's just..." She fumbled for the right word. "Too much."

Unless Vivian had somehow learned Beth's secret. Was that even possible?

Dev leveled a look at her. "Maybe she figured you deserved battle pay after being married to me. Or maybe she just thought you deserved a break."

Why hadn't Vivian said something about this?

Dev's abrupt decision to file for divorce had hurt his mother deeply—Beth had seen it in her eyes. Her former mother-in-law had remained distant but cordial whenever she stopped at the bookstore or joined the crowd lingering outside church on Sunday mornings. She'd even sent Beth a Christmas card, and included her in the dozens of townsfolk she invited for a Christmas brunch last year, though the divorce had long since been finalized.

But Vivian never made a single comment about the divorce, and there certainly had never been any hint at the contents of her will.

Beth frowned. "This must be a mistake—a forgotten clause in the will, or something."

Nora cleared her throat. "It's all legal and proper. She revised her will last February, actually, five months after your divorce was final. She went over every paragraph of it with me."

"Still, the boardinghouse would be far better managed by someone experienced in the field." Dev made an impatient motion with his hand. "Maybe a social worker. Or a nurse."

"Like I said, these were your mother's wishes. She didn't want to leave her charges to flounder without her," Nora said with a firm smile. "I'm sure she figured you would follow through."

He studied Beth for a moment, his eyes narrowed. "Maybe she had other motives."

Horror and embarrassment washed through Beth

at the obvious implication. "You think she wanted us thrown together over this?"

He didn't respond, but she could see his answer from the hard glint in his eyes. He probably even thought Beth had been in on the "plan," and there was no way to prove him wrong. Did he really think she was so needy and pathetic?

She could feel her cheeks burning. "Your mother might've had fond dreams of happily-ever-afters, but if so, she was sadly mistaken. That could *never* happen. You made that more than clear when you demanded a divorce. And believe me, I have absolutely no desire to turn back the clock."

At the force behind her words, he looked taken aback. "No insult intended."

No insult intended? He was even more obtuse than she'd thought. She took a steadying breath. "None taken. I'm just stating facts."

Nora glanced between them. "I'm guessing this is going to be an uneasy peace between you two. Maybe even impossible."

Silence stretched uncomfortably between them.

"I'll request extension of my leave," he finally said through clenched teeth. "We can make this work. Right, Beth?"

Beth swallowed hard. "If we want to save your inheritance and my bookstore, we don't have a choice."

She reached out and tried to ignore the sudden, familiar warmth that sped through her when his large, strong hand briefly enveloped hers. Warmth that triggered a rush of memories, both good and bad.

He dropped her hand as if he'd touched fire, and she knew he'd felt it, too.

They had six long months ahead.

Six. Long. Months.

The thought made her shudder, yet there was too much at stake to risk failure. And not just for herself.

Tourism had revitalized the town, but the tourists wouldn't come back if Stan pursued his business interests and destroyed the historic district in the process. If that happened, too many good friends and neighbors would suffer. The owners of the gift shops, the coffeehouses, the antique stores. Even the little marina owned by old Mr. Gerber, who'd added a fresh coat of paint to the main building just this summer.

They were all starting to prosper after far too many years of struggle, and it could all be wiped out if the quaint and inviting atmosphere of the town changed.

All she and Dev needed to do was get along and work together, and in six months everyone would have a more secure future. The shopkeepers. Vivian's last set of boarders. And Beth would even own the beloved building that housed her bookstore—something she'd never thought possible.

Dear Lord, help us succeed. Guide us in helping those people. And please, for as long as Dev is here, help me protect my heart.

Dev stepped into the Walker Building and breathed in the musty scents of mold and mice. Light filtered through the grime and cobweb-festooned mullioned windows facing the street, while the back half of the building was cast in deep shadow.

A wide, open staircase rose along the wall to the left, the wooden steps littered with crumbling cardboard boxes overflowing with yellowed newspapers and what appeared to be rags.

He'd had to come back for another look, even if his every decision would now have to be put on hold until he'd met the crazy stipulations in his mother's will.

On the endless series of flights coming back to the States and during those long days at Walter Reed, he'd had plenty of time to think, and had planned to make this trip into his past as brief as possible.

But now, the charm and peacefulness of the village called out to him with its scents of pine. The sound of Aspen Creek rushing southward over the boulders strewn through its rocky bed. The absolute lushness of the trees and undergrowth and the damp, fertile earth, so unlike the dry and inhospitable climate where he'd spent much of his adult life.

And with those scents, those sounds, came the memories he'd so carefully shelved away. Of jangling sleigh bells and the clopping of draft horse hooves on snow-covered asphalt, come Christmastime, when sleighs served as taxis for the tourists and locals who came into town for all of the Victorian decorations. The sweet, sweet scent of burning leaves and fragrant pumpkin pies and the local parade at the end of October, during the annual Fall Harvest celebration.

He stepped farther into the building and felt a sense of peace in its silence, its massive stone walls. As a child he'd loved this old building, imagining knights on chargers jangling through the stone arches that framed each door and window. Envisioning Merlin and King Arthur sitting before the immense mouth of a fireplace inside, and a damsel peering from one of the soaring stone turrets that rose above the roofline.

Now, the cavernous interior and multitude of windows spoke to him in a different way.

He closed his eyes, imagining the place filled with soft candlelight and the hushed murmurs of diners sitting at tables set with crystal and silver. Or maybe retail shelving, stocked with colorful toys, antiques or camping gear...or even trendy clothing, maybe. The stuff of fun and relaxation, and the bounteous civilian life that allowed people time to savor some of the most beautiful scenery in the world.

And he tried to imagine a time when war would no longer be a part of his life. No reconnaissance missions, no explosions. No rapid-fire, staccato blast of his M249 while he covered his buddies...or the comforting weight of an M16 cradled in his arms.

But that was reality.

Being here was like stepping into an old-fashioned Christmas card that he'd have to file away in a few months, because he might as well be visiting the moon for as much as he could relate to the breezy, small-town atmosphere where the greatest dangers were mosquitoes and the newest crop of inept teenage drivers. He couldn't even *begin* to relate to the innocent, cheerful residents who expected to go about their business unharmed every single day, then sleep safe in their own warm beds at night.

Shaking off his thoughts, he wandered through the building, trying to quell the deep sense of longing flickering to life inside his chest.

Each of the four buildings in this block were roughly the same, with thick sandstone walls built to last for centuries, and old glass rippled with age set in the tall, narrow windows. Yet each building also bore unique, whimsical details in the fanciful figures carved into the stone lintels over their doorways, the patterns of the mullioned windows on the second floors, and the ornate details in the rooflines and eaves.

He still couldn't believe his mother had risked letting any of this fall into the hands of her brother-in-law, unless she'd wanted to insure that Dev would come home to stay, so he could prevent it. Was she really that crafty? Had she no idea of how difficult it would be for him to deal with Beth? Didn't she care?

Then again, Mom hadn't really known him at all. He certainly hadn't come home much, and when he did, he hadn't stayed long. He was a far, far different person now than he'd been as a boy.

His palm still burned at the remembered touch of Beth's hand back at the law office, and his conscience nagged at him over how rude he'd been.

On the trip home from D.C. he'd dredged up a few rusty prayers over how he was going to avoid running into his ex-wife. Gutless prayers, to be sure, and since few of his prayers had been answered in battle, he'd figured that the Almighty wasn't listening anyway.

God sure had to be laughing now.

Having to face her during that meeting had left him more tense than any battle or covert operation. And now, instead of managing to avoid her and the old, raw emotions surrounding their ill-fated marriage, he was going to be seeing her all the time.

Worse, he had to do a good job of it—to insure that the stipulations of his mother's will were met well enough to pass muster with a couple of attorneys planning to guard her interests.

The irony was almost enough to help him ignore the aching in his shoulder and the sharp, stabbing pain that radiated down his upper arm with every unguarded movement.

At the sound of a knocking behind him, he spun toward the front door, automatically reaching for his absent weapon and scanning the interior of the building for exits and cover, his heart rate escalating.

He blinked.

Forced himself to relax.

And squinted into the sunlight streaming in behind a slender figure silhouetted in the windowed upper half of the door. Though the thick, rippled glass muted her shape, his gut wrenched and his heart took an extra thud at his instant recognition, triggering emotions and memories that were long dead…and would stay that way.

She knocked again, then tried the door handle and pushed the door open to stand in the entry, looking a little hesitant. "I…I was outside the bookstore and saw you unlocking the door down here. Mind if I come in?"

He gave a single, sharp nod.

Beth stepped a few feet inside. Avoiding his gaze, she surveyed the interior, her eyes sparkling. "Wow—just look at the natural light coming through all the high windows, and look at all the space. This place has tremendous potential. It ought to be perfect for whatever kind of business moves in here." She gave him a speculative look. "Maybe you should just lease it instead of selling. You might want to come home for good someday."

"No. I'll be leaving as soon as I can, and I won't be back. There's nothing to keep me here anymore."

Her expression hardened. "Of course not."

Guilt lanced through him at his inadvertent, callous words. "I didn't mean it that way."

"It doesn't matter." She raised a delicate eyebrow, making him feel like an even bigger jerk. "We've both moved on. All for the best, and all of that. Right?"

A shaft of sunlight lit her wildly curly chestnut hair, highlighting its varying shades of amber and gold. It had always felt so soft and silky, he remembered; baby fine and fragrant with the scent of wildflowers. Gentle, just like her.

She'd so deserved better than someone like him.

He belatedly realized that he hadn't answered her when her smile wobbled and her gaze slid away from his.

"I…didn't mean to interrupt, or anything," she murmured. "We can talk another time."

She wore gleaming gold hoops in her ears and a long denim skirt, topped with an oversize ruby sweater that looked soft as rabbit's fur. Despite the casual clothes, she had an air of sophistication and reserve far different from the girl she'd been years ago.

It was something he needed to remember.

They'd both changed so much. There was no going back. All they needed was to be businesslike. Polite. Focused.

"But I do think we need to talk, Dev," she added. "When you have some time."

He winced. "Uh...yeah. Some time."

She ignored his dismissal. "Maybe now rather than later, come to think of it." Her mouth flattened. "Because I think we need to make something perfectly clear."

Chapter Three

Maybe Beth hadn't much personal experience, given her absentee husband, but she'd certainly read enough of the pop-psychology books in her store to know that most guys cringed at the thought of discussing feelings. If she'd ever doubted that bit of wisdom, she only had to look at Dev's guarded expression to know it was true.

But standing here alone with him, with no other distractions, was probably the perfect place to set things straight.

"We need to talk," she said briskly, "because we need to put the past to rest, once and for all. Otherwise, this situation will be unbelievably awkward."

He studied her, his eyes wary, as if he expected her to dissolve into a tearful, wretched mess.

But she'd die before she allowed him to catch even a glimpse of the damage he'd caused…or the pain she felt, every single day, since her life had been shattered. No matter what her mother claimed, he had relinquished that right.

"I admit…" She hesitated, searching for an innocuous word that would betray nothing of how she truly felt. "That it was a shock when you insisted on a divorce. But you have your life in the service and other relationships to pursue, I'm sure. The last thing you needed were bothersome ties to a wife back home. Right?"

His eyebrows drew together.

"It didn't take long for me to get over it, really." She managed a smile, even though her heart was pounding against her ribs and the half-truth now lodged in her throat like a chunk of granite. "So don't worry about having to deal with any big scenes from me. I have no regrets."

His jaw tightened. "That's…good."

"So with that cleared up, it shouldn't be hard to maintain a business relationship with each other, right?" She fluttered a dismissive hand. "The other thing I need to clarify is that your mother's will was a complete surprise. I had no idea she'd included me, and I certainly didn't try to finagle my way into her good graces."

"I never said—"

"But you might have thought it. Just so you know, your mother was polite but distant to me after the divorce. Even before that, we were never chummy during all the times you were away in the service. There were no little chats, no invitations for coffee. So if you're imagining any sort of collusion regarding you, her will or my bookstore building, you couldn't be more wrong."

A muscle ticked at the side of his jaw. "I didn't suggest anything of the sort."

"She stayed in your corner," Beth added for emphasis. "And I didn't expect or seek anything more. Now it's your turn."

"What?"

"If you have any concerns or questions, go for it."

He fell silent, his intense gaze locked on hers, as if he were examining her very soul. "I...guess not," he said at last.

"Good. So now we can try to be friendly business associates, at least. No other expectations."

"Right."

"It's good to see you in one piece," she added. "When I heard you'd been wounded, I started praying that you'd be all right."

His gaze shifted away. "Thanks."

Years ago, he might've added a sardonic laugh at any acknowledgment of her faith, but this time he actually seemed to mean it. Yet another way he'd changed into someone she no longer knew, she mused. "So you think your shoulder will be fine for active duty?"

"It had better be," he muttered.

He edged away and she saw the glint of something at his ear. "Was...that your only injury this time?"

"Pretty much." But then he caught her studying him, and he sighed. "That, and a little hearing loss," he admitted. "Just temporary."

"I read a *Newsweek* article that said a lot of soldiers suffer permanent hearing loss because of the gunfire and explosions. Then they can't go back."

"It won't be an issue," he bit out as he strode to the entryway. "Not with me."

* * *

Though she'd told herself that she wouldn't ever waste the time, she thought about Devlin as she headed back to the bookstore.

He had caught the eye of all the girls in high school, and no wonder. But while his golden-flecked, whiskey-brown eyes and the dark sweep of his eyebrows had bordered on heartthrob handsome as a teenager, now he was at least six feet of solid muscle, and the uncompromising planes and angles of his lean face were attractive in a far more rugged way.

They'd married young—too young. They'd probably been as much in love with love itself as they'd been in love with each other. With her own rocky family life—a free-spirited, irresponsible mother and a dad she barely knew—marriage had promised love and stability, and offered the kind of security she'd rarely felt growing up.

In comparison, Dev's family had seemed like something straight out of a happy TV sitcom—parents who'd been married for over twenty years, who'd lived in the same house since before Dev was born, who lived their faith in a steadfast way. She'd imagined that when she and Dev were that old, they'd be just like them.

She'd discovered the truth much later.

Alan's ironclad expectation that Dev would achieve nothing less than straight A's in high school and then go into medicine had sparked extreme tension between them. With Alan, nothing was ever good enough…and Vivian had sided with her husband.

For coming through his teen years as balanced as he

was, given the constant criticism he faced at home, Beth had been completely impressed with Dev's strength. She'd been so sure their marriage would be a safe and happy shelter from the world.

But growing up in a cold and distant household and building a career in the military hadn't made him a warmer guy.

Then out of the blue, he'd come home from a tour in some undisclosed place, and announced that their marriage was over. No explanations, no apologies…and the next day he was gone.

He'd been a wild one, a charmer in high school, and she should have known better than to risk her heart.

It wouldn't be something she'd ever do again.

Beth eyed the antique grandfather clock opposite the checkout counter. The stately pendulum swung back and forth. Back and forth. Slower, it seemed, than ever before.

Twenty-four minutes to go, and counting.

Sauntering through the empty store once more, she straightened books and fluffed the colorful patchwork pillows strewn on the overstuffed chairs angled into every corner.

She'd let Janet, her sole employee, leave early to make it to her twins' Friday night football game in nearby Parkersville, and since then there'd been exactly two customers who'd braved the unseasonable chilly evening to stop in.

Both were frequent browsers, but the gentleman did put a heavy coffee-table book on Egyptian art on layaway, and his cheerful little wife selected several magazines while she sipped hot peach tea.

Eighteen minutes.

Beth thought longingly of the raspberry scones and hot chocolate that she'd savor upstairs in less than an hour. After today, she needed that and a good hot bubble bath, too.

Nearly two-dozen three-year-olds had run amok in the store during the morning—ostensibly for story time, though they were new to the preschool experience and none landed in one spot long enough to hear more than a few consecutive words.

As soon as they left, both Beth and Janet had flopped onto the red velvet sofa in the History section and burst into laughter.

The afternoon had been quieter, with the garden club ladies using the meeting area to discuss the town square gardens for next year.

And then there'd been her talk with Dev.

Even now, her midsection felt jittery and unsettled, though she was pretty sure she'd carried off her visit with an air of calm detachment that had conveyed none of her true emotions.

Lord, I hope You'll help me through the next six months, because it isn't going to be easy.

She eyed the clock again. Fifteen minutes to go. Good enough.

Her step lighter, she made one more sweep of the store, checking the windows and back door, then ended up at the front register where she began counting out the cash drawer.

The jangle of the bells over the front door startled her and she spun in that direction. Her mouth fell open at the rainbow apparition standing just inside. *"Mom?"*

"Sugar!" Metal bracelets clanging and overlarge hoop earrings flashing, Maura Carrigan swept forward in a flurry of multiple layers of fuchsia and peridot scarves and shawls over some sort of canary, gauzy muumuu underneath. Blond this time, her hair caught up in a twist with strands flying about her face, she was as colorful as a one-woman carnival.

Beth accepted her mother's fierce hug and hugged her in return. "You look…wonderful."

Maura grimaced. "Not really, after all those days on the road. But color always perks me right up." She held Beth's shoulders and took a step back to survey her head to toe. "My *goodness,* but you're thin."

"Not thin. Ten pounds too high, according to the charts."

"Thin," Maura retorted. "And so…so *staid.* It's a good thing I'm here."

Amused, Beth looked down. "A long denim skirt and cranberry sweater isn't exactly staid. I think I'm actually sort of Midwestern hip."

"Well, we're going to see what we can do about that, hon."

At Maura's calculating appraisal, Beth quelled the urge to roll her eyes. Her mother had embraced the flower child era with gusto, and at sixty she had yet to let it go. "I'm nearly done down here, Mother. As soon as I close, we can go upstairs. I've got the guest room ready. It's small, but you'll be comfortable while you're here."

"It's a lovely room, as I remember. Now, don't mind me. I'll just wander around the store for a while and let you finish up."

Beth watched her stroll away, the initial bounce in her step fading. Was that a weary droop to her shoulders? Despite Maura's trademark ebullience upon arrival, there'd also been something else—a trace of worry, maybe. Or stress. Two emotions she'd always said she wouldn't waste a nickel on, which made them of concern now. Was it just the long trip, or was something else going on?

Frowning, Beth finished checking her totals and filled out a deposit slip.

A minute later the door jangled again...probably Maura heading out to get her luggage, Beth thought as she dropped the money and slip into an Aspen Creek Savings & Loan night-deposit bag.

"You're closing up already? Guess I got here too late."

At the all-too familiar deep rumble of his voice, Beth looked up in shock. "D-Dev?"

"I've been thinking about what you said, and you're right on all counts." He approached the front counter with the newest Lee Child hardback in his hand, his eyes troubled. He dropped a couple of twenties on the counter. "This situation isn't going to be easy for either of us, but we'll manage. I want to apologize for being rude, and thank you for being willing to try."

She glanced over her shoulder, then rang up the

purchase and handed back his change, hoping he wouldn't linger. "Maybe we can discuss this tomorrow morning—"

But it was too late.

In a flurry of retro-hippie scarves and beads, Maura came around the corner of a bookshelf clutching a large hardback on organic gardening.

Her mouth fell open, then her eyes narrowed. *"Devlin,"* she exclaimed, her voice low and bitter as she looked between Beth and her nemesis, then pinned her glare on Dev.

"Mom, please," Beth pleaded.

"How can he have the *audacity* to come in here?"

"I think I'd better go," Dev said in a low voice. He turned to leave. "No sense in making anyone upset."

Beth watched him go, her heart heavy. Maura had been against their marriage from day one, proclaiming that it was a terrible mistake. Ever the champion for her two daughters, she'd later pinned all blame for the divorce on Dev's shoulders. Her heart had truly turned to stone over what happened after that, and Beth knew her mother would never, ever forgive him.

But the clock was already ticking on the situation with the Sloane House boarders. There was a lot of work to do with no time to waste, and much of it was going to involve Dev.

It was going to be hard enough as it was, and now Beth could only pray that she could keep her mother and Dev apart until at least one of them left town.

Chapter Four

Beth stood at the open door of her car and watched Dev park his late father's Jeep behind her bumper, hoping her mother's outburst hadn't irreparably damaged their tenuous truce.

Maura had retreated into troubled silence on the topic of Dev after their encounter on Friday night. And since Dev had never been one for emotional scenes, preferring a stony retreat to fanning the flames of an argument, it wasn't likely the two of them would ever come to any level of understanding even if they did run into each other again.

Beth had hoped to see him at church this morning for a chance to talk, but the fact that he hadn't shown up wasn't a surprise. As a teenager he'd attended only rarely and probably under duress, though his parents had been pillars of the community and staunch members of the church.

An old memory surfaced, of the first Sunday after Beth's family had moved to town. She'd been a high school sophomore, and could still remember seeing the dark, brooding teenager in a pew with his parents. He'd been tall, dark and impossibly handsome. That raw, youthful appeal had nothing on what he'd become…six feet of solid muscle, with an aura of strength, even when he was standing still.

She'd never known exactly what he did in the Marines, but had no doubt that he completed his missions with the kind of intense, lethal power that allowed nothing to stand in his way.

Now, he climbed out of his vehicle, clearly favoring his injured shoulder, and started up the walk leading to the two-story brick home where he'd grown up, pausing to stare at the discreet, forest-green sign over the porch steps with Sloane House written in fanciful gilt letters.

There was no warmth in the firm set of his jaw or the flinty expression in his eyes when he spared a brief nod in her direction.

"Cool wheels," she called out as she closed her car door.

"What?"

Belatedly remembering that he might not hear her clearly, she spoke louder. "The Jeep. It sure brings back memories."

"Dad's house calls," he said on a long sigh.

Clutching a leather folder to her chest, she caught up with him at the front steps. "He had to be the last of a dying breed. He was such an institution around here."

"A real hero, all right."

Though from the lack of emotion in Dev's voice, he'd

been one to everyone but his son. "Even if he wasn't a perfect father, he was well loved in the community, Dev."

Dev tipped his head in silent acknowledgment.

"Nora told the boarders that we'd be here this afternoon. So how do you want to handle this?" Beth asked.

"I don't. Hand me an M16—"

Startled, she looked over her shoulder at him. "A *what?*"

"Hand me an M16, give me a mission, and I'm good to go. But I don't fit this everyday life in the States anymore. So how am I going to help these folks? If my mother cared about them, she should've allowed us to hire the appropriate staff."

Beth suppressed a shudder, imagining the kinds of dangers he'd faced all these years. "I'm not sure these people *need* a staff, as such."

"Then aren't there other options—like low-cost public housing?"

"Not nearly enough in the county, and none here in Aspen Creek. The economy hit this town pretty hard over the past few years, so I don't suppose there are any plans, either."

Dev looked unconvinced. "I knew she'd turned the house into a boardinghouse, but her country club and golf buddies were her primary focus when I was a kid. I still can't imagine my mother doing this."

Privately, Beth agreed. Vivian Sloane certainly hadn't had a very warm heart when it came to welcoming a young daughter-in-law into the family. What could have made her change during the last few years?

"Well, Nora has been overseeing things since your mother passed away, and that's what her report said. Did you read your copy?"

"Just the first few pages so far."

"She explained the whole operation, and listed the current residents. We've got just four adults here, plus one of them has her young son with her."

Dev's eyebrows rose. "A child? *Here?*"

"Hey, there are homeless families everywhere. At least this mom has a safe place for her son to live."

"How long have they all been here?"

Beth shuffled through the papers in the folder. "According to the records, the current boarders moved in during the three months prior to your mother's heart attack. Elana and her son Cody arrived just the week before." She looked up and caught a flicker of uneasiness in Dev's eyes. "But good news—residents do benefit from being here, and then they do move on. There were actually two more women and a gentleman, who left a few weeks ago."

"Successfully, I hope."

"All have their own apartments now, and have jobs in town. Nora has checked in on them a couple of times." She looked up at him, and bit back a smile at the grim set of his mouth. "This isn't some dangerous mission, Dev. It might actually be fun."

"Right. If 'the blind leading the blind' isn't a recipe for failure."

"We'll do fine. I suppose we should talk to them as a group and allay any fears they may have, then meet with everyone individually. What do you think?"

He sighed.

"Ready?" She crossed the wide plank floor of the porch, noting the half-dozen Adirondack chairs and rockers with bright red cushions and a checkers set sitting on a table. At the front door she hesitated, then rapped on the door.

A few moments later, a somber, gray-haired man peered out a beveled windowpane in the door before he opened it. "You must be Vivian's boy." He gave Dev a narrowed look. "And…you must be Beth Carrigan. We've heard about things changing around here."

"We're only coming on board to help out. Right, Dev?" She looked over her shoulder and winced at his dark expression.

"Folks here are worried. Most of us have been waiting in the parlor to hear what you have to say."

"And you are?" Beth asked, extending her hand.

"Carl White. Thirty-two years on the railroad line till my heart gave out." He thumped his barrel chest with his fist. "Got a pacemaker and new valves—a real overhaul. Almost ready to go down the tracks again."

But his face was ashen, and he sucked in a rattling breath after each sentence. If he was planning to go down the road, she hoped it wouldn't be very far.

"Good to meet you, Carl."

Overhead, a massive chandelier hung in the center of the two-story entryway. Beyond lay a wide hallway flanked by a curving, open staircase with a dark, burnished oak railing.

Beth had always been as intimidated by the grandeur of the house as she'd been by her in-laws' subtle disapproval. From the stiff set of Dev's shoulders, he didn't have happy memories about the place, either. No wonder. With his mother's charitable works and active social life and his father's dedication to medicine, they'd earned a sterling reputation in town, but they sure hadn't put a priority on understanding and supporting their only child's wishes.

Carl led them to the dining room, where the original, gleaming cherrywood dining room table and chairs for twelve still took center stage.

A patrician silver-haired man, probably in his early sixties, studied them as they walked in. The austere, elegant woman across from him was a woman whom Beth recognized as an infrequent customer at the bookstore. Her upswept, coal-black hair and perfect manicure were badges of prosperity, so what was she doing here?

Carl cleared his throat. "This is Frank Ferguson and Reva Young." The woman nodded. "Our youngest residents, Elana Mendez and her boy, couldn't be here."

Beth cast a quick glance at Dev, but he shook his head slightly, turning the discussion over to her.

"As you know, Dev and I have been given the responsibility of taking over the management of this house, to satisfy the promises his mother made to each of you. Today we'd like to meet with each of you privately to discuss your concerns and needs. But first, are there any questions we should address with the group?"

Carl scowled. "About the costs…are they going to be the same?"

Wishing Dev had been more willing to discuss details out on the porch, she shot another glance at him and caught his almost imperceptible shrug, then nodded. "According to the documents I have, you all pay a flat hundred-dollar monthly rent for your room, plus a hundred for your share of the food, supplies and lawn care. We have no plans to change that at this time."

Pugnacious as a boxer spoiling for a fight, Carl sat forward with his jaw jutting, drumming his fingers on the table. "When do you plan to kick us all out and close this place?"

"The agreement you all had with Vivian was for a six-month stay—renewable based on need, on a case-by-case basis. Her will stated that should she pass away, the full six-month period would start fresh for everyone living here."

"Then what?"

"We'll do our best to help you all get a good start at renewed independence," Beth assured him. "Just like Vivian did. No one will be thrown out in the street. If there are problems, we'll talk. However, this was never intended to be a long-term boardinghouse."

Beth felt a tug at her heart when Carl nodded bleakly. For all his crotchety bluster, he was *afraid*.

What *would* happen to these people if successful independence wasn't attainable within six months, or even a year? Yet…what could happen to the viability of this entire scenic tourist town if that didn't happen, and Stan Murdock got his hands on the property?

Would Nora and Harold be ruthless in their application of the terms of Vivian's will and let Stan lead the town to ruin?

After fielding a few more questions, Beth and Dev moved to the parlor across the hall to meet with the residents individually. With each passing hour, Beth's concern grew. Was it even *possible* to meet the stipulations of Vivian's will?

Carl was a childless widower with no family to watch over him. Asthma and advancing congestive heart failure had led to his early retirement at fifty-six, a minimal railroad pension and little stamina for the only kind of blue-collar work he knew. He was regaining his strength after a subsequent heart attack but now, at fifty-eight, was he even able to be self-supporting? And would anyone actually hire an older man with such a dour outlook on life?

Reva Young came in next. At close range, her perfectly coiffed black hair revealed a hint of silver at the roots. Her bearing was regal as she settled into a chair and folded her hands primly in her lap. The tight compression of her lips and her white knuckles betrayed her anxiety.

She eyed the leather folder on the end table next to Beth's chair as if it were a snake ready to strike. "I suppose you have information on all of us. Is there really anything at all left to say?"

Beneath the acid tone, Beth heard a glimmer of fear. "Vivian wasn't a social worker and neither is the lawyer. There's no social history or deeply personal information on anyone—just the most basic information, plus old addresses, recent work history and emergency contact information. Exactly what you filled out on your application before moving in."

"I see."

"What are your goals?"

"I...have degrees in French and Comparative Literature." Her lower lip trembled, though she met Beth's gaze squarely. "I'm afraid that doesn't translate to many career choices in the Northwoods of Wisconsin."

"You haven't ever worked, then?" Beth asked gently.

"My late husband was a banker, dear. He did quite, quite well." If her voice grew any colder, it might splinter into crystalline shards on the Persian rug beneath their feet, and now a note of bitterness crept in. "I spent my life supporting all of his endeavors."

"So...do you have some ideas about what you'd like to do?"

The woman's chin lifted defiantly, and Beth guessed that she was hanging on to every last shred of her pride.

"I...don't know. At fifty, with no résumé..."

But if her husband had done so well, what was she doing here? The obvious question hung between them for a long, uncomfortable moment.

"I don't mean to pry, Mrs. Young. Dev and I just want to help."

"My husband should have played our portfolio conservatively as he got older. But he took big risks thinking he was going to make a killing, then several significant dips in the stock market nearly wiped us out. He ultimately left me widowed with a heavily mortgaged home, a lot of debt and almost nothing in the bank…and trying to ignore rumors that he hadn't even been faithful. Ironic, isn't it?" Reva rose gracefully to her feet. "The banker's wife turned pauper sounds like such interesting fiction. But in real life, it's a grand disappointment, and rising from the ashes, as it were, will be no mean feat. I know I need to find a job, and I'm trying. I'll keep you informed."

Beth waited until she heard the woman go up the stairs, then shook her head. "I feel so sorry for her."

Dev shifted in his chair. "Makes you think, doesn't it?" he said in a low voice. "Good health and a regular paycheck are quite a gift."

"True." *And a family support system, too,* though Beth didn't say those words aloud.

She still had her mom and a sister who both lived on the West Coast, but as an only child with both parents gone, he no longer had any close relatives she knew of. And yet he'd thrown away their marriage as if it had been worth nothing.

Had he been unfaithful, like Reva's husband?

Not long after the divorce, Vivian passed her on the street and offhandedly mentioned Dev's advantageous new relationship. Had he been having an affair before the divorce was even final? That possibility had once made her heart twist with grief.

It would certainly explain why he'd been so brusque, so emotionless the day he'd asked for a divorce. He'd left town quickly after delivering that devastating statement, then was off again into the Middle East for an extended tour of duty. He'd resisted all her efforts by e-mail to try to save their marriage.

Though if he'd had someone else in the wings, apparently that new relationship hadn't worked out either, because he sure seemed to be alone now.

Frank appeared at the arched opening to the parlor with a thick manila folder in the crook of his arm, a faint red flush at his neck in stark contrast to his snowy hair. "So you want to know when you can boot me out, eh?"

Beth looked up at him, relieved to see a brief flicker of humor on his lean, sad face. "No booting. We're only trying to see where everyone stands, and what we can do to help."

"Well, I'm the oldest fogey here, at sixty." He took a chair across from them and folded his hands on top of the folder he'd settled in his lap. "I don't know what any of us would've done without Vivian's boardinghouse. When this place closes…" His voice trailed off as he stared at his hands.

"That's a long ways off," she said gently. "I understand you were a teacher. Did you enjoy it?"

"It was my *life*. I never married, you know, so teaching meant everything to me. Seeing my students succeed gave me great satisfaction."

"What happened?"

"Falling enrollment. Consolidation of two school systems. I should have been secure after so many years, but the school closings meant that many of us were simply let go. I lost my home when I couldn't keep up with my mortgage payments." He offered a wry smile. "If one happened to buy during the real estate boom up here, it was very bad news when the market plummeted."

"Have you looked for other teaching opportunities?"

He leaned forward to hand her the folder. "Take a look."

She thumbed through the stack of papers, all copies of job applications he'd filled out. "You've been *busy*."

"I've applied for every teaching position I qualify for, bar none, in a four county area. For two years I've come up completely dry. But that's not a surprise. I was fifty-eight when I lost my job and a teacher with my years of experience is more expensive to hire than one just out of school, you know. So—" he gave a little shrug "—here I am."

"What about other types of careers?"

"With only small tourist towns around here, there's mostly just seasonal work in the summer, and even that has taken a hit lately, with the economy and all. I do have a part-time job at the library, but that's just a bit over minimum wage." A rosy flush colored his gaunt cheeks, revealing just how much the admission cost his pride. "I want to work, but I'm a useless old man before my time, I guess."

Beth considered her words carefully. "Have you considered places farther away? Larger cities?"

"As a last resort. I've been here almost since I was a boy, so to leave lifelong friends, family and a place I love, well..." He splayed his fingers on his thighs. "But if I have to, yes."

Dev had been silent during the other interviews, but now he cleared his throat and surprised Beth by leaning forward, his elbows propped on the arms of his chair and his fingers laced. "Have you thought about a different career entirely? With your teaching experience you might be excellent in business. Sales, marketing…"

"I have, actually. I'm going to take some accounting classes starting spring term at the community college." Frank smiled. "I never thought I had much of a head for business and numbers, but I'm going to give it a try. Maybe someone, somewhere, will give a hardworking man another chance. If I could work until I turned eighty, I'd be the happiest man alive."

At the end of the afternoon, Beth walked with Dev to the street, feeling the weight of lost dreams and flagging hopes weighing down her shoulders like a heavy, sodden cloak.

She stopped at the sidewalk. "I guess I don't know what to say," she murmured. "It's all just so sad."

Dev jingled the keys in his jacket pocket. "There are people in worse shape, though. No place to live, worse health."

"True. I just…" She searched for the right word. "I just want to *fix* everything right now, because everyone looked so worried. All of them have been honestly trying to turn their lives around. So how can we assume that we can make a difference?"

"We can't be miracle workers. This place is an opportunity for them, and the responsibility is theirs, too." He lifted a shoulder. "Six months is a long time."

"And what's the deal with Elana? Everyone was so guarded when we asked about her. It was like…like they were *protecting* her."

Dev frowned. "If she's in trouble, we need to know. It could put this program and everyone in it at risk if we're harboring someone running from the law."

But that *someone* had a young child with her, and the thought of a homeless child tugged at Beth's heart. "Your mother vetted these people. I don't think she would have taken in a fugitive."

"We can hope." Dev lifted a hand in farewell as he continued walking toward his Jeep. "See you around."

She would never pursue a romantic relationship with him again. Or anyone else, for the foreseeable future, because she now had so little to offer. Yet Dev's casual dismissal still felt like a direct hit in the vicinity of her heart. "Where are you staying—in case I need to contact you?"

"The Starlight Motel."

"Why not the guest cottage behind your parents' house?"

He sighed and turned back to look at her. "Because I expected to be on my way in a few days. This place doesn't hold a lot of good memories for me, in case you've forgotten."

"But—"

"But now…I guess I'll have to consider it."

She took a step back and craned her neck for a glimpse of the matching redbrick cottage behind his family home. She'd once thought it as charming as a dollhouse, with its crisp white shutters and gingerbread trim, but now one of the shutters hung askew and the little house had an air of sad neglect. "If it's going to take a lot of work in there, I—"

"If it needs work, I'll take care of it. You're busy enough as it is." Sparing her a brief smile, he pivoted and headed toward the Jeep, his long stride and military bearing masking the shoulder injury that surely had to be bothering him after so many hours of inactivity this afternoon.

With a sigh, Beth glanced at her watch as she turned for her own car. As a brush-off it had been tactfully delivered. Twice, in fact. And in truth, she'd buried her pride to offer help, but greater proximity was not for the best.

Still, a small part of her felt a twinge of disappointment. It was only human nature to want to be helpful, even to a stranger. Especially if that person was injured or hurting in some way. And though he didn't mention it, that shoulder had to give him consider pain. But... so be it.

The bookstore was open from one to five on Sundays during tourist season, though it would close in an hour and Janet could handle that. Maura was probably pacing Beth's upstairs apartment, eager to go out together so they could visit some of her old haunts with whatever daylight was left...and keeping her busy would be infinitely better than staying at home, where she might start back on the topic of Devlin Sloane once again.

As Beth climbed behind the wheel of her car, she closed her eyes for a moment. *God, these next months aren't going to be easy. Please help Dev and me get along, so we can do our best to help those people. And if You can, please soften my mother's heart.*

Chapter Five

I handled that meeting so *well,* Dev growled to himself as he drove through town the next morning. He'd thrown common courtesy out the window, with someone who'd only wanted to help.

Your ex-wife, a small inner voice reminded him. *The one you treated so badly, only a year ago.*

He cruised slowly past the bookstore. Debated about stopping to apologize…then remembered that Beth's mother was probably inside, her claws bared.

Why the woman seemed to bear such a serious grudge after all this time wasn't hard to fathom, but she certainly didn't try to hide her feelings. Where was her Christian sense of forgiveness? His parents had certainly held that concept dear, at least on the surface.

Then again, maybe it was just as well that Beth had her guardian mama around.

He sure didn't have any plans to stay in Aspen Creek. Even if he did, he had no business thinking about her, and surely he was the last man on earth she'd ever want to spend a minute on, anyhow.

He'd seen the stark pain and shock in her eyes when he walked out on their marriage. Her frustration when he'd refused to even listen to her attempts at salvaging their relationship…though he suspected her efforts were because of her deeply held beliefs about the sanctity of her marriage vows, rather than any deep feelings for a man as damaged as him.

War had changed him in more ways than she could ever know, with her genteel life of books and friends and pleasant customers.

And whether she believed it or not, he'd done her a favor by leaving her behind.

Dev pitched another shovelful of debris into a refuse barrel. Renewed pain lanced through his shoulder, forcing him to lean on the shovel and take long, slow breaths.

The town he'd been born in now felt as foreign as some distant planet, where the inhabitants expected security and happiness, where their day-to-day lives centered on inconsequential issues and they fully expected to be alive and whole twenty-four hours from now. That false sense of safety was as incomprehensible to him as the culture of iPods and BlackBerrys and home video games that had swept this quiet part of the world during his absence.

But he *would* succeed in meeting the stipulations of the will. Murdock would be out of luck.

And then…well, Beth would own her building and be

safe from greedy developers like Stan, and the rest of the buildings could be sold to people who would *preserve* the historical flavor of the area. End of story.

Yesterday, Dev had headed straight to the Walker Building after the meeting with Beth, just to lose himself in the mindless, backbreaking process of clearing out the interior, and today he'd come back for the same reason. It wouldn't hurt to start cleaning it out at any rate, so he could leave town faster when his six-month sentence was up.

An excellent plan…except this morning, it had taken two ibuprofen and a couple strong cups of coffee to get himself moving. Still, hard physical labor was better than dwelling on the past…and every street corner, every gracious old mansion and quaint storefront of Aspen Creek seemed to trigger memories he'd tried to forget.

That first date at the ice-cream parlor with Beth, the spring of his senior year in high school, when he'd just turned eighteen and she'd been a shy, sweet junior— prettiest girl in the entire school.

The old mom-and-pop-run theater, now boarded up, where he'd first held her hand and eventually found the courage to ease his arm around her slender shoulders.

The endless walks they'd taken along the quiet streets of this small, historic town, with canopies of elm and oak overhead and the fragrance of flower beds drifting from manicured yards…streets that now reminded him of the hopes and dreams he and Beth had once shared. Dreams of a perfect life, perfect home, and two or three perfect children.

Naive dreams of happiness not yet touched by war and death, and the harsh reality of life.

So much was the same here—yet there'd been changes, too. Back then, many of the stores were failing, victims of a struggling agricultural economy and the exodus of people toward better jobs in the Twin Cities to the west, and Madison to the southeast.

Now, Main Street boasted art galleries, upscale gift shops, and high-end specialty stores through the center of town, while many of the fine old homes at either end of Main now housed bed-and-breakfasts, antique stores and restaurants. Parallel to Main, Hawthorne ran for several blocks along sparkling Aspen Creek, and in between the blooming array of touristy cafés, coffeehouses and artisans' shops at the northern end, one could catch glimpses of the towering, rocky cliffs on the opposite bank of the creek.

In the block owned by the Sloane estate, only Beth's bookshop was open for business, but that would be changing once he got the other buildings sold.

Though by that time, he would be back to active duty and long gone, if sheer perseverance counted for anything.

The physical therapists at Walter Reed had recommended a series of strengthening exercises to work on every day to maintain mobility in his shoulder joint and build his strength. Each day he tripled the recommended number of reps, then added more of his own.

With that, and working on the building, he was going to be ready to rock by the day his medical leave ended. A day that couldn't come too soon.

"Yoo-hoo," a voice warbled from the open front door. "Can I come in?"

He turned toward the entryway to find a tall, slender woman with silver hair cut in a short, almost masculine style standing in the doorway. "Can I help you?"

She stepped inside. "Do you remember me?"

It was a question the locals liked to ask, though it had been so long since he'd lived here and so much had happened during the intervening years, that he struggled with names and faces. A decade of physical changes made it all the harder.

He knew this woman, though. He shifted uncomfortably as he tried to place her wry, friendly smile and that light silver hair.

"Olivia Lawson. I believe," she added with a twinkle in her eye, "that I was your third-grade Sunday school teacher."

Fourth, he remembered, as his mind locked onto the precise memory, though he didn't correct her. Her hair had been a glossy brown back then, and she'd had the ability to quell the rowdiest behavior—often his—with a single, piercing glance. She'd also been a great storyteller, able to hold her classes rapt with the way she could make a Bible lesson come alive using her dramatic voice.

Another dim memory surfaced. "Weren't you an English teacher, too?"

She smiled. "Community college—and still teaching. I was also an acquaintance of your mother's, through church."

Less pleasant memories, there.

She cocked her head, studying him. "I hear you've led quite a life of adventure."

He stiffened, waiting for the hint of censure that he'd always heard as a teenager from those in his mother's social circle, where the adults engaged in subtle games of one-upmanship when it came to their children's career choices. Greetings directed at him invariably drifted into questions about his plans to follow in his father's footsteps…or would it be law instead of medicine?

Exactly the expectations his family had held for him, until he'd rebelled at the recruiter's office. His parents had never failed to let him know of their disappointment in him after that, whether through subtle comments or long-suffering sighs.

He spared Olivia a brief nod, then scooped up another shovelful of debris.

"We're all proud of you, you know—and your service to our country. Our pastor names each of our local men and women in the military during our Sunday prayers."

At the unexpected note of approval in her voice he paused and looked back at her. If any of the hometown folks had ever noticed his absence, much less been proud of him, his family hadn't chosen to relay the information. "Thanks."

She surveyed the area, then tapped a finger against her lips. "You should get some help, or this cleanup will take forever."

"I've got the time."

"The youth group at the Aspen Creek Community Church could do it in a snap," she said decisively.

"They're always looking for fundraiser projects. Buy them pizza, make a donation to their program, and you'll have this cleaned up in no time. Though given who your mom was and what she did for them, they'd probably come for free."

What she did for the *youth group?* At *church?* Olivia had to be confusing Vivian Sloane with someone else.

She laughed aloud. "From your expression, I get the feeling you didn't know your mom very well in her later years."

"I haven't been around here much since I enlisted. We…didn't always see eye to eye."

"Something she always regretted, no matter what you might think." Olivia drew closer and rested a slender hand on his shoulder. "I believe she once said that you two were too much alike."

He stifled a snort at that. Country club events and golf tournaments had certainly been his focus all right, to the exclusion of everything else…like a bothersome child.

"I think she mentioned 'stubborn' and 'independent' once or twice, but my memory could be wrong." Olivia winked. "I guess I'd better be going. Maybe I'll see you in church Sunday?"

He shrugged. *Not likely.*

She waggled the tips of her fingers in farewell as she left, leaving him to count the number of times he'd been asked about church in the past twenty-four hours.

Barring a few of the newer people in town, everyone he'd encountered seemed to recognize his name whenever he stopped at a store or gas station. They offered condolences about his parents and dredged up pleasant-ries about how much they were missed in these parts. And then they assumed Dev would be slipping into the traditional Sloane pew, right up front.

But he'd seen too much, learned too much over the years to ever be able to resume that falsely pious family role again.

Maybe God watched over the good folks of Aspen Creek, but He sure hadn't followed Dev to the Middle East or into the halls of Walter Reed. And if He hadn't stepped in when Dev had needed Him most, He certainly wouldn't care about what happened now.

The cell phone on his belt clip vibrated. He lifted it and glanced at the caller ID, trying to ignore the instant rush of awareness that he'd tried to forget. He almost said a silent prayer for strength, before he caught himself.

It was *Beth.*

At the sharp rap on the door of Beth's office at the back the bookstore, Elana grabbed for her son and retreated to the corner of the room, dragging him with her. Their dark eyes widened with fear, even though Beth had told them Dev was on his way.

The door cracked open a few inches. "Beth? What's going on here—" Dev pushed the door farther open, caught sight of the cowering woman and seemed to instantly assess the situation. He stepped inside, closed the door and offered her a disarming grin as he eased into one of the other chairs. "I'm Vivian's son, Devlin Sloane. I'm guessing that you must be Elana Mendez?"

The woman managed a single, jerky nod.

"She couldn't meet with us yesterday, so I called and asked if she could stop here after work." Her hands clasped on her desktop, Beth leaned forward to smile warmly at the seven-year-old by the woman's side, praying that Dev wouldn't telegraph surprise or pity when he got a closer look at the boy's twisted leg and the gaunt, slight appearance he and his mother shared. "And this is her handsome young son, Cody."

If Dev noticed anything unusual, his expression didn't betray his thoughts. "Nice to meet you both."

"I'm glad you got my text, Dev. I thought it might be good if we talked together, as we did with the other residents...just so we're all on the same page." Beth tilted her head at Cody. "If all this grown-up talk is boring, I know Janet has a plateful of chocolate-chip cookies you two could share."

Elana bit her lower lip as she glanced uncertainly between Beth and her son. "I don't think...well..."

"The store is quiet right now. I can ask Janet to stay with him in the children's area. It used to be an office, so there's just one entrance. She could even shut the door."

After a long pause, the young woman nodded and said something to Cody in rapid-fire Spanish, though she watched pensively when Janet came and led him away slowly enough to accommodate his pronounced limp.

When they were gone, she slipped into an empty chair as far as possible from Dev, where the fluorescent light overhead now picked out premature silver strands in the long, dark hair that she wore twisted into a tight bun. "I...worry for him." She bowed her head over her folded hands. "And for us."

When Beth looked up and exchanged glances with Dev, she felt her heart falter at the frightening intensity of the cold, hard anger and resolve that blazed in his eyes before he looked away. He was clearly ready to do battle with whomever Elana was frightened of...but how could he wage war against the ghosts in her past?

Beth hesitated as she searched for the right words, feeling more out of her league than she'd felt with any of the other residents of Sloane House. *Lord, help me say the right things here.*

"I understand if you want me to go," Elana whispered into the moment of silence. She shifted uneasily in her chair, as if she were getting ready to flee. "I know the boardinghouse is not meant for children. I don't want trouble for anyone."

"That's not what we want. Not at all." Beth infused her smile with an extra measure of warmth. "We want you and Cody to stay. We just want to know what your goals are, and how we can help."

The woman's furtive glance at Dev nearly broke Beth's heart. Just in these few minutes, it hadn't taken long to guess at what lay in Elana's troubled past.

"I...I have a job as a maid. At the motel. I am saving money so I can go to school someday." The expression in her eyes turned bleak. "But...it is taking a very long time."

The motel on the edge of town had seen far, far better days, so the wages they offered were surely nothing above the minimum level. Beth rested her chin on her upraised palm and tapped a finger against her lips. "I wonder if there would be better jobs, for someone who is so fluently bilingual. Maybe at one of the resorts outside of town, or the bank?"

Elana sat forward in alarm. "No. No—the motel is fine. The hours are good. I take Cody to school and walk him home. Always."

Dev nodded. "It's safer that way."

"*Sí*...I mean *no*." Flustered, Elana's gaze darted between them as she reached blindly for the battered purse by her chair and started to rise.

"Wait." There was no mistaking the command sheathed in his gentle tone. And though he hadn't moved a muscle toward her, she sank back into her chair. "Is this about an old boyfriend?"

She white-knuckled the handle of her purse.

"A husband, then?"

A single tear slipped down her cheek. "Roberto was no good. He...hurt Cody."

And Elana too, Beth thought with growing anger at the man who had gotten away with victimizing the family he was supposed to love and protect. What kind of animal was he?

A muscle jerked at the side of Dev's jaw, betraying his similar thoughts. "Does he know where you are? Will he try to find you?"

"No. He went to prison last spring."

"Because of what he did to you and Cody?"

She shook her head sadly. "Armed robbery and he

wounded a deputy. He will be gone thirty years, on federal charges."

Yet she still seemed frightened of her own shadow.

Dev turned his chair to face Elana, leaned forward, and gently took her shaking hands in his. "Then whatever happened to you in the past will not happen again. Understand? Roberto is gone. You are with friends, Elana."

She'd stiffened and dropped her gaze when he drew close, but now she shot a brief, wary glance at him.

"You didn't deserve whatever he did to you," Dev continued gently. "A man who would abuse his family deserves to be in prison for that alone. Forever, as far as I'm concerned. But you don't need to live in fear—not anymore. Now you can make a good life for you and your son. So he can grow up to be a fine man, with a good future."

Beth watched them, surprised at Dev's sensitivity and relieved when Elana's tense shoulders began to relax. "He's right, Elana. We want to help you achieve that, in every way we can."

But when Dev released her hands and stood, Elana instinctively flinched, as if none of his words had even registered.

And Beth knew that reclaiming this poor woman's courage was going to be a long, long road.

Chapter Six

Replacing a leaky faucet at Sloane House shouldn't have required much talent or time.

Fixing it with two older gents offering both running commentary and plentiful advice, plus one stern woman watching him with a hawk-eyed glare lest he run off with the dish soap, added a whole new dimension to the project.

But it was the wide-eyed boy hiding in the shadows who held Dev's full attention.

Cody's expression was still wary. Yet despite that brief encounter at the bookstore yesterday, when his mother had freaked out at Dev's arrival, there was curiosity and even a hint of longing in those dark eyes—as if he wanted to draw closer but didn't dare.

Since coming back to Aspen Creek, Dev had fended off most of the friendly overtures that had come his way, more comfortable in self-imposed isolation than at the prospect of blending into the fabric of a community he couldn't wait to leave. What would be the point, after all?

Protecting the vulnerable, fighting for justice, and putting his life on the line were pretty much the limits of his skill set, but there was something about Cody that he couldn't ignore.

"Hey, kid," he called over his shoulder as he knelt in front of the open cabinet under the kitchen sink. "You look plenty strong. I could use some help. Got a minute?"

From the corner of his eye he saw Cody waver, then shoot a hesitant glance at Carl. When Carl nodded to him, he edged forward, still keeping a careful distance.

With the wrench in his hand, Dev gestured toward the old toolbox he'd found out in the garage. "Can you hand me a wrench the next size up from this one? Here—take this one over to compare."

The boy limped forward and gingerly sorted through the toolbox, withdrew a wrench and offered it with both hands.

"Perfect—first try. Thanks, buddy." Dev finished installing the sprayer hose, then rocked back on his heels and stood. "Let's see if this works. Want to give it a try?"

Cody leaned across the sink and grabbed for the sprayer nozzle.

Carl chuckled. "Careful!"

Too late. A spray of water shot from the nozzle when Cody's hand tightened around it, catching Dev square in the midsection. The boy jumped back as if he'd touched electric wire, his face a mask of shock and fear.

The kitchen was chilly and the water was ice-cold. But his automatic exclamation of surprise caught in Dev's throat at the expression on Cody's face—as if he expected to be backhanded, or worse.

There was a moment of utter stillness, with Frank, Carl and Reva's attention riveted on Dev.

He laughed, breaking the tension. "I wasn't planning on a shower quite yet, but that's okay. What do you think, Cody—want to help me pick up the old parts? Maybe you can help carry them outside. I'll bet you know where the toolbox belongs, too."

Cody stood frozen for a heartbeat, then he rushed to pick up the old washers and faucet parts, and went out the side door leading into the garage. Dev lifted the toolbox and started after him.

Frank and Carl both nodded in approval and patted Dev's shoulder as they stepped back to let him pass by.

"You'll do," Carl said under his breath. "You'll do just fine."

Even Reva wore the faintest trace of a smile.

"Just like your daddy," she murmured. "He was a good man."

Carl's gentle touch and words of praise had felt almost like…a benediction. But Reva's burned at the edges of Dev's heart.

The old fear was still there, an ember that had never faded. And just to make sure it never had a chance to grow, he had long since made a decision.

His first marriage had failed. He wouldn't risk

another. And he definitely wouldn't ever have children, because the thought of turning into his critical and demanding father made his blood run cold.

With a large FedEx delivery of books to sort through, a steady stream of customers, and a long lunch with Maura at the Dancing Lily tearoom on Main, Tuesday had flown by.

Beth glanced at her watch as she walked in the door of the bookstore. "It's already three o'clock, Mom. I can't believe we stayed at the Lily so long!"

"It was those fabulous sour cream scones with lemon curd. I couldn't bear to leave a single crumb on the plate." Maura slipped off her sparkly purple wool shawl and tossed it over the back of an oak rocker by the front desk. "Of course, catching up with the news around here was even better."

At the wistful note in her mother's voice, Beth felt a flash of concern. "Maybe it's time for you to move here again. You always said this was one of your favorite places to live, and you still have friends here. I'd like it if you didn't live so far away."

Maura flipped a hand dismissively as she paused at the aisle filled with a long magazine rack. "They say you can't really go home again. People change, you change. It wouldn't ever be the same. And I've got a very good life in California."

But did she? Despite her tendency to flamboyance, Beth had caught moments when her mother looked pensive and distracted, though she refused to discuss it. And she was getting older, even though that subject was *strictly* off-limits.

As time went on and her health failed, what then?

"Think about it, anyway. Are you still planning to go upstairs for a nap?"

"As soon as I find a new magazine to take with me." Maura moved farther down the magazine aisle and out of sight. "Something on decorating, I think. While I'm here, I could help you spruce this place up. More vibrant colors would do it. Purples. Reds. A splash of canary. More pizzazz."

From behind the front counter, Janet grinned at Beth as she handed over a stack of pink telephone notes. "You had five messages as soon as you left for lunch," she said as she handed them over. "Three of those people called again during the last five minutes, hoping you'd returned. Olivia, the pastor, and Dev."

Beth blinked. "Goodness."

Maura reappeared. "It's a shame you need to deal with him at all."

There was certainly no problem with her mother's hearing where Dev was concerned. "The pastor?"

Maura ignored Beth's lame attempt at humor. "Your ex-husband, as you well know. But as disappointed as I am in that man, I still hope you've had that talk with him."

Beth flinched, all too aware of Janet's curious appraisal. *"Mother."*

Glancing between them, Janet tactfully slipped from behind the counter and hurried toward the back of the store. "I'm going to the storeroom to unpack some books," she called out over her shoulder. "Yell if you need anything."

"Sorry," Maura murmured, though she didn't look particularly contrite. "So...have you had that talk?"

Beth lowered her voice to a harsh whisper. *"No."*

"The last thing you needed was for that Devlin to show up in town. After the way he treated you, I hope he never does again. But he should still have to share some of the pain you went through. He deserves to know, honey."

"Does he? What possible good could that do? Nothing would change. I don't *want* anything to change. He and I are finished. Forever."

"But—"

"No, Mom. Think about it." Her voice had risen on its own, and she took a steadying breath. "He could feel remorse, and then he'd have that burden to carry. Or he might not care at all and just offer some empty platitudes—and then *I* would feel worse. Much, much worse, because I'd be so angry. And I don't know if I could ever let it go."

In her teens she might have stormed away and slammed her bedroom door for satisfying closure to the discussion. Now, she just sighed. "So please, just don't bring this up again. Promise? None of my friends know, either, and I want to keep it that way."

Maura studied her sadly. "It's your choice, so I'll say no more....except that you're wrong about this, and I hope that someday you'll see that I'm right."

Always the last word. Beth bit back a reply and

focused on the message slips in her hand. "Some of these are for you, Mom," she said as she handed them over.

Maura stared out the front window for a moment, then looked down and studied her messages. "My gallery, every last one of them. Hollister should be able to handle everything just fine without calling every two hours." She lifted her shawl from the rocker and slipped it over her shoulders with a flourish as she headed for the door. "I'll call her on my cell from upstairs."

Beth waited until her mother left, then went to the storeroom and braced a hand on the door frame. At Janet's bemused expression, she shook her head. "Thanks for the space."

"She certainly does hold a grudge—over whatever he did." Janet fanned her face with one hand. "Whew."

"My mom is a wonderful woman in many ways, but she doesn't like Dev and has never hesitated to remind me." Beth sighed. "During the years we were married, I never discussed any problems with her. She would have jumped on them like a dog on a bone."

"And what's with her assistant? This was her fourth call since your mother got here."

"I'm beginning to wonder. Except for the topic of my ex-husband, she has seemed so...so vague about what's troubling her. But I know something is—I can feel it."

"Maybe she's in the midst of some major art sales? Trouble with difficult artists?"

Beth bit her lower lip. "I doubt it. She carries very nice originals, but not major names. She enjoys giving newer artists exposure by giving them space for their shows, and then the public has a chance to get in on the ground floor with some of their pieces. Everybody's happy."

Janet held up her hands, palm up. "So...what does that mean, exactly—ground floor?"

"The oils are usually less than five hundred, the pottery and art glass less than a hundred."

"Which is about what you find in the galleries around town. So if she did move here, she could easily fit right in."

"True. And coming back to town would be a good thing. I'm worried about her, really...I think something's wrong and she just won't admit it." Beth reached for the cell phone in her purse. "And my mother can be one very stubborn lady."

Dev got out of his Jeep to study the building next to the bookstore. The lawyer had arranged to get him the keys so he could do a quick walk-through inspection.

As always, the bookstore caught his eye, and he found himself wondering if he might catch a glimpse of Beth through the big plate-glass front windows...though this time, he saw Maura coming out the door.

She stared at him. Hesitated. Then beckoned.

This couldn't be good.

But when she beckoned again, he sighed and crossed the street. At the age of thirty-four, he felt like a schoolboy being brought into the principal's office.

She moved a few yards down the sidewalk, out of sight from the store windows. Her expression was troubled. "Look, you and I have had our differences over the years, even if they were mostly unspoken. Since I'll only be here another week or so, I...well, I thought I'd better just come out and say it." Her voice was flat, without anger, but he had no doubt that she meant every last word. "I've been worrying about you spending time with my daughter."

No one could say Maura didn't speak her mind. The irony was that his own parents hadn't approved of Beth any more than Maura had approved of him. "We only have a business relationship. Nothing more."

"But my worry is that I *saw* the look in your eyes when you came into the store."

What look in his eyes? Dev jammed his hands into his jacket pockets. "Your daughter has no interest in resurrecting a relationship with me, believe me. And that's not what I'm after, either."

"I don't want her hurt her again."

"I never meant to let that happen. But she has already moved on. She has a good life—far better than she would've had with me."

"A good life?" Maura's gaze riveted on his, as if she were daring him to feel the pain he'd caused. "Someday, you two need to talk about this."

Her quiet vehemence startled him. "We have."

"No..." Maura bit her lip, as if she were debating saying more, but then she sighed. "Leave her alone, Devlin. Don't try to have a little fling with the past, then fly off to wherever it is you go these days. I have to trust that you're a better man than that."

But the expression in her eyes showed that she didn't trust him at all.

* * *

Beth's phone messages on Tuesday had all been about the same topic—setting up a youth project for cleaning up the Walker Building.

Olivia and Pastor Jamison had been brimming with enthusiasm, while Dev apparently wanted to fend them off so he could continue down his solitary path—preferring silence and slow progress to a legion of teenagers eager to do a good deed.

When Beth finally convinced him this morning that gracious acceptance was the fastest way to satisfy everyone and then be left alone, he'd grudgingly agreed.

Now, Beth stood with him in the center of the building on Wednesday evening and watched two dozen teens hauling the final garbage bags of refuse down the open stairway leading to the second floor. As industrious as a legion of ants, they'd already cleared the first level, leaving a squadron to scrub the filthy hardwood floor with scrub brushes and buckets.

"I told you this was a great idea," Beth said, slapping her dusty gloves against her jeans. "They're just about done. What they've finished in four hours would have taken you *weeks*. And you're helping them raise funds, to boot."

Dev snorted. "Not if they have anything to say about it. So far, Pastor Jamison and the kids have refused payment, other than the delivery of pizza and pop that's on its way right now."

She looked up at him and fought the urge to brush away a fragile cobweb drifting across the deep waves of his hair. A tender move that would be entirely too intimate and wifely, past boundaries she had no intention of crossing. Ever.

"Did they say why?"

"Apparently my mother grew generous in her old age. She funded one of their youth trips to the Twin Cities last year and donated money for their choir robes the year before." If he'd said that Vivian had flown to the moon, he couldn't have sounded more mystified by her generosity. "So now they want to return the favor."

"That's sweet." She hesitated. "I know you and your parents didn't get along so well when you were in high school. And...I know they weren't fair. But maybe they changed, later. Or maybe they had a good and giving side that you didn't see."

"Possibly." He hitched his good shoulder. "But I'd still rather pay the youth group and keep things square."

She lifted her hands in frustration. "Then send them an anonymous donation, in care of the church. I'm sure they can put it to good use."

He nodded. "I'll do that."

At the weariness in his voice, she looked up at the pallor of his skin and the fine lines of tension bracketing his mouth. If he was in pain she knew he'd never admit it, even if it robbed him of sleep and made each day a struggle.

Whatever military code of honor he subscribed to, it allowed no admission of weakness of any kind.

"How is your shoulder?"

"Good."

No surprise there. "And how are things at the motel?"

"Fine."

"Clean? Comfortable? Quiet?"

"If I'm not in a tent in some desert, it's all good."

"That's not exactly a ringing endorsement. How are the midnight trains?"

That earned a wry laugh. "Right on time. Every night."

"And the four a.m.?"

His half smile faded. "Ditto."

After being there over a week, she could only imagine how it felt to be shaken awake at all hours by fifty-car trains rumbling past, a few dozen yards from the motel. Especially when he needed the healing balm of deep, restful sleep.

"So when are you moving into the cottage?"

"As soon as I get time. It works just fine as a storage shed, now."

"In other words, it's packed to the rafters with odds and ends." She flashed a bright smile at a lanky teenager carrying a garbage can bristling with a full load of scrap wood. "Hey, Ryan. Would you kids be up for another project this weekend? It's the guest cottage behind Sloane House—"

"That isn't necessary," Dev cut in sharply. "But thanks anyway."

The sandy-haired boy glanced uncertainly between them as they stared each other down, then he shrugged and continued on his way.

"You don't have to be stubborn about it, just on principle," Beth hissed. "I was only trying to help."

Dev waited until the boy disappeared out the front door. "Thanks, but I don't *need* help."

"The kids could clear that cottage out in an *hour.*"

"But I already paid for the full week at the motel, and I'm in no hurry to move at any rate." Dev's narrowed eyes fixed on hers. "I don't remember you being such a take-charge kind of gal."

"I'm sure you don't remember anything at all about me." The words stumbled from her lips, unbidden, driven by the raw emotions that she'd tried to hide since Devlin had come to town. "Look," she added tersely. "I live alone, and I run my own business. And I just want everything to go just as smoothly during our brief partnership. That's a reasonable expectation, isn't it?"

He nodded, eyeing her as if she were some roadside bomb that might explode any second.

Around them, there was a bustle of activity. The banter and laughter of teenagers. Dev stood still as granite with a faraway look in his eyes, oblivious for a long moment.

He finally sighed. "You're right."

She'd been ready to argue another point, and his quiet words took her aback.

A chorus of whoops and hollers rose from the four corners of the building, followed by the sound of thundering feet as a herd of teenagers ran down the stairs to meet a delivery girl standing in the doorway with a stack of pizza boxes in her arms.

"That didn't take long." The tense set of his jaw relaxed, probably in relief at the interruption. "Excuse me—I need to pay her. Want some pizza?"

Beth shook her head.

Pulling his wallet from a back pocket, he strode to the delivery girl and smiled as he handed her three twenties, then he helped her lay out the pizza boxes on a makeshift table set up between a couple of sawhorses.

It was the first time in years that she'd seen him offer such an unguarded smile without the filter of the emotional baggage he carried.

It was a smile that deepened the laugh lines fanning from the corners of his eyes and the deep creases bracketing his mouth, and her heart kicked in an extra beat. She'd been so entranced by his deep dimples and his innate charisma years ago. He'd drawn her like no one else ever had…and she'd fallen completely, irrevocably in love…

Well, maybe not as irrevocably as she'd once thought. She closed her eyes, willing that image to disappear.

Despite everything that had happened before and after he'd walked out of her life, he still had the power to affect her as no one else ever had, and that was so unfair.

At a tug on her sleeve, she opened her eyes and found a teen with a high, bouncy ponytail staring at her with a worried expression.

"Are you okay, Ms. Carrigan? You look kinda pale. Are you dizzy? Maybe you should sit down."

Dizzy…pale…

Beth could believe it, but sitting down wasn't going to help. What she needed right now was *distance*. "I'm fine. You'd probably better get over there and grab some more pizza before the boys wolf it down."

"If you're sure..." The girl hesitated, then ran over to join her friends who were digging into the pizza boxes.

Maura had been right when she'd said it was a shame that Beth had to deal with Dev all over again...but not for the reasons she'd imagined.

Dev had shattered Beth's life long ago, far past repairing, but there was a small part of her that still hadn't let him go.

Maybe it *was* better to tell him the truth. She would find the right time...one of these days. She'd gather her courage, and once it was over, she could finally, completely erase him from her heart.

A wave of anxiety roiled through her midsection at the thought. Anxiety that would build and build and rob her of sleep the longer she waited. Maybe, she needed to get it over...

Tomorrow.

Chapter Seven

Devlin pulled to a stop in front of the old motel, stared at the dreary row of units with the cheap, ill-fitting front doors and potholed dirt parking lot and felt his skin crawl.

He'd stubbornly stayed here too long, despite the peeling paint, the musty curtains and the black mold creeping across the bathroom ceiling, unwilling to take the next step and move into the cottage.

A move that had seemed chillingly final, somehow, as if returning to the address where he'd grown up would weld him to this town forever.

But now, he thought bitterly as he looked at the envelope on the dashboard, it was all a moot point.

He'd resigned himself to six months in the States. But one trip to the Twin Cities and one twenty-minute appointment with a harried young doctor at the VA had just changed his entire future, and there wasn't a thing he could do about it.

Not one single thing.

He slammed his palm against the steering wheel. Stared at the cockeyed number 16 drooping dead center on the motel door in front of his bumper. *What am I going to do now, God? What now?*

That last explosion in Iraq had sounded the death knell on his career, and he hadn't even heard it because of the instant, *permanent* damage to his hearing that compounded what he'd suffered before. Hearing aids or not, he would never again qualify for the Force Recon team that had been his life…and his shoulder had been blown out too badly to ever manage more than basic civilian life.

Ironic, because he *had* no civilian skills, unless someone needed to keep a sniper handy or needed to mount an offensive or covert ops against a feisty neighbor.

He leaned his head against the headrest and closed his eyes against the bleak images of what his future would hold.

The Marines didn't want him, unless he chose to work as a trainer or man a desk somewhere…and after fifteen years in action neither sounded even remotely appealing.

But how was he going to start over when nothing else mattered?

At a loss, Dev paced his musty motel room, then changed into old jeans, running shoes and a faded Wisconsin Badgers T-shirt and went outside to run, ignoring the flare of pain in his shoulder with each stride. At the end of the block he took a right, crossed the railroad tracks and headed out into the country.

The deep valleys and rocky, towering bluffs were ablaze in ruby, molten gold and brilliant orange set against the dark pines, the air so crystalline clear that it almost hurt to breathe.

He pushed himself until his muscles burned and his lungs ached, then picked up an even faster pace when he reached the turnoff for the state park outside town.

The narrow park road wound through a forest, then up a sharp grade until opening on the highest point in the county. His heart pounding, he braced his hands on his knees and drew in deep breaths, then walked out the soreness in his muscles as he surveyed the patchwork quilt of rolling land spreading out in every direction.

Dense forest, brilliant with a kaleidoscope of rich reds and oranges and yellows. Sparkling streams and azure lakes, twinkling in the midafternoon sun. Black-and-white dairy cattle in emerald pastures with crisp white fencing and red, hip-roofed barns.

Whenever he tried to imagine heaven, he'd always come back to remembered images of the lush, pastoral beauty of western Wisconsin.

And now he was here, trapped by the stipulations of his mother's will and facing even greater circumstances that were out of his control. If he'd ever entertained the thought God might still be in his corner, it had now been proved wrong.

If he'd been just six feet farther away, he wouldn't have been so badly injured. He'd still have the career he loved. If his men had been farther away, they'd still be writing home to loved ones and complaining about the food and joking with each other at the base, instead of lying in their graves.

Surely an all-powerful, loving God could have interceded just that much.

If He cared.

With a bitter laugh, Dev performed a couple of quick stretches, then started down the park road to head back to town at a blistering pace, wanting to feel the pain, and the endorphin high that would follow.

Reaching for one good thing in this terrible day.

Back in town, Dev staggered to a halt, his muscles and lungs burning. Despite the cool, crisp October air, his T-shirt clung to his back and sweat rolled off his face.

Swiping at his forehead with the back of his wrist, he looked around and realized that he'd slipped back into old childhood habits and had ended up in front of his old home. *Sloane House,* he corrected himself silently. It hadn't been his home for a long, long time.

"Now, that looks plain miserable to me."

At the sound of Carl's familiar, crotchety voice, Dev straightened and looked over to find the old guy standing on the porch, his hands braced on the railing. His dark mood started to lift at the sight of Carl's perpetual scowl.

"Feels good," he called. "Join me?"

"Only if I want to die."

Dev choked back a laugh. The old codger was as cantankerous as they came. "We can't have that."

Someone was sitting in the shadows of the porch and

now stood to join Carl at the railing. Reva, he realized, when a beam of sunlight hit her pale face.

"If you've got a minute, we could use some help," she called out.

He glanced at his sweat-stained T-shirt and muddy running shoes. "I'll go change and be right back."

"No need," she said archly. "The attic isn't the cleanest place around."

He dutifully jogged up the porch steps, then followed her and Carl up to the second floor. At the landing Carl paused to catch his breath, while Reva marched around the corner and ascended the much narrower steps leading to the attic. At the top she flipped on a switch for the three bare light bulbs hanging from the rafters.

"I have a trunk and some boxes that need to go to my room, if you don't mind. I need my fall wardrobe for an interview coming up." She pointed them out. "While you're up here, maybe you'd like to take a look at your parents' treasures."

Treasures. More like outdated clothing in mothballs, he guessed, but he dutifully followed her to the far wall of the cavernous attic, where stacks and stacks of boxes had been stored, along with a great deal of dusty furniture.

His childhood desk and bed. Why had his parents kept them?

The beautiful old dining-room set that had come from his grandmother Lydia's home.

A surprising number of end tables and whatnots. Sofas and overstuffed chairs, and large, mysterious pieces that loomed in the shadows.

Reva lifted an eyebrow. "Did you know this was all still up here?"

"Not a clue," he admitted. "And I have no idea what to do with it all."

"Well, you'll need furniture if you use the guest cottage. I don't suppose you'd want to buy anything new, since you're going back into active duty when you get done with us. Right?"

Her words slammed his thoughts back to his appointment this morning, when the doctor's casual words had changed his future in the space of fifteen seconds.

She rested a slim hand on his shoulder. "I'm sorry— did I say something wrong?"

"No."

Her thin, softly wrinkled face furrowed with concern. "I'm afraid you aren't very convincing. I promise that we aren't as hopeless as we might seem. Every one of us *is* trying to move on."

"It isn't that." He shifted uneasily, hating the thought of discussing anything personal. Despising his own weakness. But the worry in her eyes deepened and he had no choice but to elaborate just to reassure her. "I… was just thinking about my appointment at the VA, is all. I can't get back into active service…quite as soon as I'd hoped."

"Oh, dear." Her hand fluttered at her throat. "I hope you'll be all right. If there's anything—"

"Nothing. Nothing at all." He wheeled around and picked up her trunk, then started for the stairs.

"Wait—maybe you shouldn't be carrying that after all," she called out as she trotted after him. "I can handle it...."

And now his life had been reduced to hearing a fiftysomething woman offer to carry a trunk because she thought he was *disabled*.

He gritted his teeth against the gnawing pain in his shoulder and silently continued down the stairs to the door of the second-floor master bedroom suite, where "Reva" had been engraved on a brass doorplate.

She reached around him and pushed the door open. "Anywhere is fine." She worried at her lower lip. "I can get the others, really."

"It would be a sad day if I couldn't do this much," he managed through clenched teeth. "I'm *fine*. And I'm supposed to be helping *you*, remember?"

He loped back up the stairs and brought down both boxes in one trip, settled them on her bedroom floor and dusted off his hands. "Anything else?"

"No, nothing at all," she fretted, eyeing him with considerable worry. "I just hope this wasn't too much for you."

Dev felt heat climb up the back of his neck. He could handle himself in combat, but fluttering, hovering women were so far beyond the scope of his experience that he was at a dead loss at how to respond.

"The boy is fine," Carl barked. He rose from the settee under the window at the top of the stairs leading to the first floor. "Don't send him off—there's plenty to do around here. Someone needs to move my favorite chair, because it's all wrong for the TV. He can check out the dryer vent…and there's a broken screen on the back porch. And if he's got time, I could use a ride to the shoe shop over on Willow. Sam is slow as molasses, but surely he has my oxfords resoled by now. He's had 'em for two months."

"Carl," Reva snapped. "Can't you see—"

"If the boy can go out running, he isn't an invalid. Plain as day to me." Angling a keen look at Devlin, Carl pursed his lips. "Unless he don't have time."

"No problem." Relieved at the opportunity to escape, Dev nodded at Reva and headed downstairs. "Just tell me what you want me to do first."

His life was in ruins. Old people pitied him. And now he'd gone from commanding a unit of skilled marines to becoming a jack-of-all-trades—and an incompetent one, at that.

What did he know about appliances and civilian life skills—and how was he supposed to help these folks at Sloane House turn their lives around, when he couldn't even manage his own?

Reva, with her polite but brittle, imperious shell, was so far outside Dev's years in the military that she might as well have come from a different planet.

Cantankerous as he was, Carl was at least familiar ground. If the man had chosen the military and ended up a drill sergeant, he would have been the happiest man alive.

So far, the sofa, a settee and two upholstered chairs had nearly worn trails in the carpet while Carl dithered and barked orders. The first half hour had been amusing. The second had become more than a little trying.

"No," he growled. "I just wish I could do it myself. Over more to the left. No—too far. Back to the right. Just you wait—someday you'll have trifocals and a bad heart, then see if *you* can ever get things right for watching your TV."

Carl's offhand words were harder to take than this endless exercise in furniture positioning.

Dev already had his hearing loss and bad shoulder. Was this where his life was headed? Was he going to end up growing old alone, bitter and cranky—still young enough to work but unwanted? At a point where the minute adjustment of a piece of furniture was a major issue?

The prospect darkened his mood even further, until he felt as if a heavy cloud was pressing him down into a morass of despair. He'd never understood depression. He'd always figured emotions were a choice. Now he wasn't so sure.

"Devlin."

He blinked and shook off his thoughts.

Carl frowned at him. "You moved it too far."

"Yes, sir." He adjusted Carl's favorite easy chair a few millimeters to the right. "How's this?"

Carl settled into the chair. Squinted at the television. Tipped his head up and down. "That'll do," he said. "Now, about the dryer vent. Just how much do you know about dryers?"

Only that he'd always done his laundry at the base or at a Laundromat when he traveled, and that someone else kept the machines working. And that with anything he tackled, Carl would question his every move. "Not much."

Carl gave him a measuring look. "I think it's the sparrows again," he said finally.

"Sparrows?"

"Clothes won't dry. Happened before—fool birds built nests in the vent to the outside. Jammed everything up, lint and all. Vivian called a repair guy once, then later she did it herself."

"What?" Dev tried and failed to imagine his elegant mother in coveralls, a greasy wrench in her hands. Maybe the old guy was hallucinating.

"She used a clothes hanger. Made a big hook and dragged it all out." Carl scowled. "I'd do it myself, but I can't bend down that far, and Frank has his asthma—all that dust and lint really set him off last time. No use spending good money on a repairman if this will solve the problem and we can do it ourselves."

At the reading of the will, Dev had imagined needing to be some sort of pseudo social worker here—which would have been a classic case of the blind leading the blind, since he had more than enough baggage of his own. These people would probably see through him in a minute, if it came to that.

At least *this* stuff was easy.

Carl grabbed a wire coat hanger from the front closet and unfolded it as they went outside, then rounded the side of the porch to the dryer vent. "Here you go. And don't step on the hostas."

"Yes, sir."

Sure enough, there was at least one bird nest and a mass of lint backed up inside. In ten minutes Dev had it cleaned out, then he ran to the basement and turned on the dryer. A rush of hot air soon came through the outside vent.

"Good enough," Carl said with a grudging look of approval. "Long overdue, but good enough."

An image of his father's stern expression flashed into his thoughts. *An A- in trigonometry? Maybe next time you can work a little harder. You missed a spot with the lawnmower—daydreaming again?*

Back then, he'd clenched his teeth and quietly taken the criticism, knowing from long experience that it was nearly impossible to earn unqualified praise from the man everyone else in town held in such esteem.

Now he gave Carl a level look. "I didn't hear about it until this afternoon. If you'd told me sooner, I would have come over."

"Yes. Well. Of course," Carl blustered. "I…we just didn't know. We…didn't figure you were happy about your mom's will and all, and you haven't been here much."

Had he seemed as surly as *Carl?*

Unapproachable?

At this rate the residents would have plenty to complain about if Nora or that other lawyer stopped by, and they would have good cause.

"I just figured someone would call if they needed anything." Dev cleared his throat. "I'll start coming to the house every day from now on, just to check in. Maybe we should also have a clipboard inside the back door so you can all leave me notes. Would that work?"

Carl nodded slowly.

"But I've got to admit something you probably already know," Dev added. "Give me a weapon and a mission, and I'm good to go, but there's a lot of home maintenance that I've never done before. So if you have any advice, I'll be glad to hear it. Mostly. Even if my pride gets in the way."

"Deal." The old man's voice cracked, revealing just how much it meant to him to be useful, and a moment later his mouth softened into what might pass for a rusty smile.

"I'll jog back to the motel to get my car. Then let's take a look at that screen before we go after your shoes, okay? Maybe we can drop it off at a hardware store to be fixed."

At the motel, Dev changed into khakis and a navy polo shirt, clipped his phone to his belt and climbed into the Jeep. The motor roared to life when he turned the key.

His phone rang.

He palmed it, read the ID screen and felt his heart take an extra hitch. "Beth."

"I...um..."

The residents were wary of calling him, and he'd been too self-absorbed to even notice. Now he could even hear a hint of wariness in Beth's voice, and he felt a stab of regret.

"What's up?"

"Well…I heard that you got some news today."

He tightened his grip on the phone. Reva or Carl must have called her the moment one of them was out of sight. He felt an instant surge of rebellion at their interference.

That news revealed weakness. Failure. And it was nobody's business but his own.

"Dev?"

"It's nothing."

"Then you shouldn't sound so angry."

He took a deep breath. "I'm only angry at myself. Not you."

She was silent for a long moment, obviously waiting for him to elaborate. "I hear you didn't get medical clearance for going active again."

He stared at the faded paint and torn screen on the motel unit in front of the Jeep. Just being here made him feel depressed. Maybe that was it—it was just the motel. He'd be able to handle everything else once he moved out of here.

"This is like pulling teeth, you know." She cleared her throat. "Look, I want you to know that I'm sorry. You've been hit with a lot of trouble recently, and it just isn't fair."

"Fair isn't a word I've been using much lately."

"So…give me details."

"My shoulder. Hearing loss."

"Is this forever? Are you out of the service for *good?*"

He gripped the phone tighter. "Only as far as combat is concerned. I can continue in some other area."

"*If* you choose to re-enlist," she said softly. "But you'd hate being in some office job."

"What else am I going to do?" The words came out more harshly than he'd intended. "The Marines have been my life since I was nineteen. And even here—how am I supposed to be able to help those people at Sloane House when my own life is a mess?"

She fell silent for a minute. "I was sorry to hear the news, Dev. But now I'm even more sorry."

He felt an uneasy, guilty prickle at the back of his neck, already knowing what she was going to say. Already knowing she was right.

"I understand it's bad news. So be it. You've still got so much more to be thankful for. Your vision, your mobility. Your *life*. You are so lucky. And your parents have left you resources beyond the dreams of most people. Even if you don't want to live here, you could do a lot of good in this world with that money."

"You're right."

"I'll give you twenty-four hours. But if you dare wallow in disappointment longer than that, then believe me. I'm—" She broke off suddenly. "Oh."

"I'll do my duty here. Then I'll go back to the Marines and finish out my career. Who knows...maybe after that I can go back to school, or figure out some sort of business."

"Like security, or law enforcement?"

"I just don't know. Not yet."

"Maybe you'll even decide to come back here, then. It's a wonderful town, Dev. And for as long as you'll have been gone, it could still feel like a fresh start. Where else would you go?"

Good question.

He no longer had ties anywhere on the planet...no longer had anyone who cared where he went, or what he did. He'd lost touch with his more distant relatives years ago.

But while that had once made him feel free, now it just made him feel...empty.

Chapter Eight

After a sleepless night, Dev downed a couple cups of black coffee at a truck stop on the edge of town, then got back into the Jeep and drove aimlessly through town... only to find himself turning onto Hawthorne.

He continued down to the end of the block, nodding at the folks strolling along the sidewalk who waved at him—which, it seemed, approached just about a hundred percent of the people he saw.

The first few days, he'd been uncomfortable at the recognition and attention from veritable strangers. Now he realized that they were all simply an incredibly friendly lot, and waved to everyone.

Pulling to a stop in front of the Walker Building, he rested his wrist on the top of the steering wheel as he surveyed the beautiful old building and once again imagined a rainbow of colorful kayaks leaning against the exterior wall, and an American flag fluttering from the empty flagpole angling skyward from the second floor above the entrance.

Was it even possible? Not likely. If he sank his savings into a business like that, he'd probably end up broke before the year was out.

At a sharp rat-a-tat against his half-lowered window, the world around him exploded. His heart rate escalated to triple speed, his focus narrowing to a single point—survival.

He lurched to the right, twisting within the confines of the tight space behind the wheel as he automatically reached for his gun.

A gun that wasn't there.

Panic surged through him as he pawed at the dashboard. The passenger seat—

An angular male face framed in a furry bomber cap, his features blurred with sags and wrinkles, stared through the window at him with a startled expression that had to match his own.

It took Dev a moment to recognize Frank Ferguson, one of the boarders.

The man adjusted his tie and tapped at the glass again. "You okay in there, son?"

"Fine. Just fine." *Until you nearly made my heart stop.*

In this lazy, quiet community, Dev perceived the threat level as low. He'd relaxed his guard. But it took almost nothing to bring the past crashing back on him with the lethal force of an AK-47.

Once again, images of blood and death crowded into his brain. His hands started to shake.

The acrid scent of gunfire and smoke filled the air, making it impossible to breathe.

It isn't real. It isn't real.

Taking a slow, steadying breath, he curled his fingers around the steering wheel and tightened his grip until his knuckles turned white.

When he opened his eyes he found several passersby on the sidewalk had slowed and were bending over to look through the passenger side of the Jeep with expressions of concern.

"Is everything all right with this man, Frank?" A heavyset woman in an orange jacket frowned. "He looks white as a sheet."

Her friend's eyes widened. "Oh…this is Vivian's son, right? Is he okay?"

He hadn't blushed since he was a kid. Maybe not even then. But now Dev felt heat rise at the back of his neck.

Frank straightened. "Of course he's fine. We're just visiting." Under his breath, so only Dev could hear, he added, "Old friends. They mean well, but they're busybodies. Sorry about that."

Dev opened his door partway, letting the elderly gent step aside, then he got out, needing to escape the oppressive confines of the vehicle. "I…I was just checking out my building. What are you up to?"

Frank arched his spine, one hand at the small of his back, then unbuttoned his suit jacket. "Morning constitutional. I walk three miles twice a day, no matter what the weather or I stiffen right up. Sunshine and exercise do the trick."

The innocuous conversation felt like a healing balm to Dev's raw nerves. "Must be tough."

"Shouldn't happen at my age, but there you are. I'm only sixty, but I got my white hair by fifty, and I even needed a hearing aid when I hit forty-nine—just like my dad." Frank gave Dev a piercing look. "But I'd guess things aren't so easy for you either, eh?"

I'm fine had been his constant refrain since coming to Aspen Creek and he started to say it again, then stopped, all too aware that Frank had just witnessed his meltdown a moment ago and would know it was a lie.

"You're hoping to return to active service?"

"I…was." Saying the words aloud once again made them even more painful. More real. "The VA says I have permanent hearing loss and a bum shoulder. I won't ever qualify again for my old unit."

"I don't suppose you want to ride a desk somewhere."

"No, sir."

"Just Frank. And I don't blame you. I imagine you've had to see and do things that most people couldn't…but having to leave that adrenaline rush behind would seem empty, somehow." Frank stepped up on the sidewalk and studied the front of the Walker Building. "I always admired the architecture along Hawthorne. Could you show me the inside of your building, if you've got a minute? I haven't been in there for years."

Relieved at Frank's tactful change of topic, Dev rounded the bumper and went to unlock the front door, then ushered him inside.

The older man moved to a wide square of sunlight beaming through the windows on the second floor and turned slowly, taking it all in. "I always loved this building. Nice and open in front, clear up to the rafters, but the back half will give you extra space on that second floor. And it's rustic—just the kind of interior that fits the historic district."

Dev nodded.

"I think there was a lawyers' office in here, some time back. A person could come in here and put in offices or a store in no time flat." Frank strolled through the main floor. "Build some shelving, order merchandise and you'd at least have a start at some income—then the whole winter to finish it right. Looks like you did a fine job clearing it out."

"Thanks to the youth group at church. And Beth," Dev added with a short laugh, "who wouldn't let me say no to them."

Frank pinned Dev with a measuring look. "She's a good woman."

Dev knew where the old guy was heading, and wanted no part of it. "Have you ever seen the lower level?"

"Can't say as I have. Is it just storage?"

"Not any longer." Dev led the way to the back of the store and punched a button. "There's a nice, wide flight of stairs, but we'll take the freight elevator down."

When they reached the lower level, Dev flipped a bank of switches and light filled the cavernous, empty space. The walls were sandstone block, the floor stone. The youth group had helped him remove the last of the junk down here as well, and as he headed for the series of garage doors forming much of the east wall, Dev felt a familiar tug of excitement.

He opened them one by one, letting in a rush of crisp fall air. "Take a look."

Frank joined him, and when he reached the open doors his jaw dropped in awe. "This is beautiful."

Aspen Creek widened along the stretch behind the block, sunlight sparkling in eddies and swirls as it danced around several boulders and swooped under a downed tree.

Massive old oaks, lacy birch and aspen on both sides of the creek blazed ruby and orange and vivid yellow, all the more striking against the backdrop of granite cliffs rising behind them on the far side of the creek.

Frank moved to the edge of the creek and sat on a boulder the size of a sofa. "So…what do you plan to with this place?"

"No plans."

"No, really." Frank grinned. "Don't tell me you haven't given it a thought."

Dev shrugged. "I should sell it, when I take possession."

"But…"

Dev laughed. "You are one insistent man."

"That's because I'm intrigued. I saw the look in your eye when we walked through this building—and your expression when you opened all these doors."

"Well…I guess I've been imagining an adventure sporting goods place here. Someone might be able to establish a good business, if the economy doesn't falter too much. Then again, it would be a huge risk to even try."

"And down here?"

"Kayak and inner tube rentals. Customers could practically step outside the door and go right into the water. Of course, there'd have to be van service of some kind for return transport." Dev felt a glimmer of excitement building in the pit of his stomach. "Rock-climbing gear, cross-country and downhill ski equipment...there could be something for every season." Dev cleared his throat, a little embarrassed. "For whoever might be crazy enough to take the risk, that is."

"Crazy? Sounds like a great idea to me. Of course, I never did get into all of that sporting stuff," Frank said with a wistful smile. "I'm just a stuffy old man who wouldn't know a kayak from a duck boat."

"It's not too late."

"Even in my younger days I wasn't all that coordinated." Frank gave a self-deprecating laugh. "So...if some *stranger* was to pursue that dream of yours, what might he do with that strip of land between the back of the building and the river?"

"Picnic tables, maybe, so customers and staff could come out and have lunch. Think it would work?"

"Sounds great. How soon can you open?"

Dev choked back a startled laugh at Frank's subtle persistence. "Like I said—"

"Sounds like you've been doing a lot more thinking about this than you realize, son. If I were you, I'd put a pen to paper and see if it's possible. How hard could it be? You need a new career. This building is yours—or it will be—and it's perfect."

"You make it sound easy."

"Maybe not easy, but it could be a lot of fun. New

beginnings can be a grand adventure." Frank pursed his lips. "I've found that praying hard on something helps guide me in the right direction...unless God has better plans. You oughta give it a try."

"Now you sound like Beth."

Frank gave him a keen, penetrating look. "Well, she's a believer, and she's a young woman who set out to accomplish things on her own and did them well. So I guess I'll take that as a real compliment."

Back up on the main level, Frank followed Dev out onto the street and watched as he locked the door.

Dev hesitated. "I have to admit I thought about this place last night, when I couldn't sleep. I kept thinking about display cases, and merchandise, wondering if it was even possible."

"Well, I can tell you that there's not another business like it within twenty miles of Aspen Creek, and the tourist trade has been increasing every year. Good steady business all summer long, and they expect at least twenty thousand visitors during Fall Harvest weekend. Last year, they came from a hundred-mile radius. Not bad for a little town like ours."

"I'll give it some thought."

"Good timing," Frank mused. "The Fall Harvest Festival is in two weeks. If you get on it, you could put in a few display cases and racks, and at least bring in a little merchandise to showcase your plans for the future. That could really get some word-of-mouth going for you, with all those people trampling through."

"Sounds like a great idea, but I don't know where I'd even begin...and that's not much time."

Frank rocked back on his heels, rubbing his chin as if deep in thought. "You wouldn't need to get the whole place pulled together by then. But some nice big outdoor sports posters might be just the ticket."

Dev stepped back toward the curb and studied the front of the building. "And bright flags out front—with a few colorful kayaks leaning against the wall."

"And it wouldn't take that much to get started, inside. Shelving, some displays. Figuring out what to order would be the hardest part, but I might just know someone who could give you some tips. After the festival, you could work on getting stocked in time for winter sports, and you'd have all winter to do the place up right and be ready for spring."

Dev laughed. "You are a *dreamer*."

"Of course, it's a big job for one guy. If you decide to go ahead and need some help, a few hours a day with a screwdriver or hammer wouldn't kill me. Not for pay," Frank added quickly. "I'd just be returning a favor. I'm sure you'd rather be anywhere else than this quiet town, riding herd on a bunch of older folks."

Dev felt a flash of guilt. It was true, and he couldn't think of a single thing to say in response.

"Days get a little long when you don't have a job and can't find one that suits," Frank added into the long silence. "But I'll understand if you don't want anyone in the way."

With the exception of the bomber hat he liked to wear, Frank looked like an elegant old guy, and he was certainly well-spoken. But the melancholy in his voice revealed the toll his situation has taken. "No luck with the job hunt, I take it."

"I sent out another two résumés this week. But one look at my long years of experience, and anyone can guess my age. Yet I'm too young to retire, and have too many good years left to want that. And I will *not* consider public assistance."

From the first moment he'd heard about his role in his mother's last wishes for Sloane House, Dev had planned to do only what he had to, while guarding his personal distance from the boarders.

Camaraderie could save your life, but real friendship only led to sorrow when a good buddy died in action. Over the years he'd lost too many, and he'd developed a tough hide and an instinct for emotional survival.

But Frank, with his stubborn pride and the way he painstakingly dressed up each day in a well-worn suit and tie, as if doing so might help make his own dreams come true, was a man Dev was beginning to admire. "Maybe I could use help. An employee."

A corner of the man's mouth lifted in a wry smile. "I didn't mean to play a sympathy card, son. I don't know the first thing about all this high adventure outdoor stuff. I'm just an old man talking."

In coming here today, Dev hadn't meant to open a store, much less offer a job, but the unbidden words had tumbled out of his mouth. Yet now, the possibilities in front of him sounded better by the minute.

"I'm going to crunch the numbers, like you suggested. If it looks good, I'll let you know." Dev felt his excitement over the idea growing. "But I sure couldn't do it by myself."

"Well…" Frank hesitated, though the new sparkle in his eyes gave him away. "Then I guess I'm your man. Just say the word."

"I know you're looking for a better career than this, though. There'll be no hard feelings if you come across something else."

Sirens wailed in the distance. Faded, then grew louder as they wound through town.

Frank's snowy eyebrows drew together. "There's a sound I never want to hear. In a small town like this, all too often they're coming for someone I know."

Both men turned toward the sound. A second later, an ambulance careened around a corner several blocks down and came roaring up the street, its sirens deafening and flashing lights blinding as it skidded to a stop in front of Beth's bookstore.

Beth? Frozen in place for a split second, Dev stared. And then he started to run.

Chapter Nine

"Help is here," Beth said, gently placing a throw pillow under Janet's head. "You're going to be just fine."

"I'm just glad there aren't any customers here. If I'd landed on someone…" Janet groaned, her hands protectively laced over her belly and her eyes closed. "I can't believe I did this."

"It could happen to anyone," Beth soothed. She looked up expectantly when the front door crashed open and two fresh-faced young EMTs rushed in.

"She twisted her ankle." Beth stood and stepped back out of their way as the two young women knelt at Janet's side. "She fell over that step stool by the bookshelves. She didn't want me to call nine-one-one, but I was concerned about the baby."

The blonde, with "Teresa" embroidered on her shirt pocket, checked Janet's pulse and flashed a penlight at her pupils while the brunette pulled out a stethoscope. "How far along are you, ma'am?"

"Seven months." Janet looked up at her with a faint

smile. "My teenage boys think I did this at my 'advanced age' just to embarrass them."

The bells over the front door jangled again, and this time Dev burst through the door. He surveyed the situation, watching the EMTs continue their initial assessment for a moment, then he turned to Beth and gently gripped her upper arms. "I heard those sirens and thought something had happened to you."

Flustered, she met the intense, searching expression in his eyes and tried to smile in return. "Sorry, but you're still stuck with me for the next six months."

He made a sound of frustration deep in his throat. "That isn't what I meant, and you know it."

The bell over the door rang as more people crowded inside. Frank Ferguson. A few of her regular customers. And, Beth realized with chagrin, her mother.

Maura frowned as she quickly dismissed the woman on the floor and glanced between Beth and Dev. "What's going on here?"

Beth took a step back to release Dev's hold on her. "Everything is fine," she called out to the gathering crowd. "Janet just took a little fall."

"But you're all right," Dev said in a low voice. "Thank God for that."

"I do thank Him. Every single day." She turned back to Janet and the EMTs. "Is there anything I can do?"

One of them was talking rapidly into a cell phone. The other one double-checked the air splint they'd just placed on Janet's left leg, then sat back on her heels. "We'll be taking Ms. Baker in. She needs to be seen by a physician."

Beth held a hand at her throat. "Is it serious?"

The EMT shook her head. "That's confidential, ma'am."

Janet lifted her head a few inches, her skin pale. "They want to make sure the baby is okay," she whispered. "My husband is out of town. Would you call my sister, and let her know? She can tell the boys."

"Absolutely. I'll follow you to the hospital, if you want me there."

"That would be wonderful. If anything happens to this baby..." Janet's lower lip trembled. She turned toward Teresa. "Please, can she ride in the ambulance with me?"

The EMT hesitated. "Well...there's room, as long as you're stable."

"I'll follow," Dev said, resting a hand on Beth's upper arm once more. "I can wait with you and then give you a ride home."

Maura drew in a sharp breath. "I could go instead."

Beth looked between Dev and her mother, feeling the exponential rise of tension sparking between them. "Mom, this could be a long wait, and you said you didn't sleep well last night. Dev can help me out."

Maura looked between the two of them, then her gaze locked on Devlin. She gave a reluctant nod.

With rhythmic precision the EMTs positioned the gurney next to Janet, transferred her, then raised it with a clang. After looping thin, clear oxygen tubing over her head and adjusting the nasal cannulas beneath her nose, they pushed her out the door.

* * *

"Gracious," Frank murmured as he watched the ambulance pull away from the curb. "You just never know."

Dev nodded, feeling a twinge of guilt at his relief over the fact that it wasn't Beth lying prone on that gurney. "Janet must be in her early forties, but she looks healthy enough. She'll probably be home in no time."

"Maybe." But the hint of sadness in Frank's voice belied his words.

"Is she a good friend?"

"No, I just see her at church. Nice gal."

Dev frowned at Frank's grim expression. "Then what is it?"

"Just…remembering." Frank's shoulders sagged. "I think I'll finish my walk, if it's all the same to you. If you see Janet at the hospital, tell her I'll be praying for her."

Dev jingled the keys in his pocket as he watched Frank start down the sidewalk with a heavy step, all evidence of his upbeat mood over his new job gone.

At Frank's age, he'd probably experienced plenty of loss…parents, friends, maybe siblings. Accepting the cycle of life for all its joys and sorrows didn't make it any easier. And without a wife, facing the inevitable, inexorable increase in losses as one grew older had to be a lonely business.

Exactly what Dev knew he'd experience himself someday, alone. Unless he managed to get back into active service again, and some random sniper or chance roadside bomb in the Middle East got to him first.

* * *

Dev found Beth in the Trauma Center waiting room, her arms folded across her midsection. As usual, her hair had escaped its tidy knot and wild, chestnut tendrils curled at the side of her face giving her a look of vulnerability.

Vulnerability brought into sharper focus by Maura's earlier words of warning still ringing in his ears, and the realization that holding Beth's arms for the brief moment in the bookstore had reawakened more than just a landslide of memories.

He'd felt the same electricity, the same sense of completion he'd felt with her all those years ago. And how was he going to deal with that now?

Distance.

Beth's obvious relief was palpable when he walked into the empty waiting room, and he felt a flash of guilt. "Where's Janet?"

"I got to be with her in the E.R., but now they're doing some sort of tests. Her sons and her dad got here a few minutes ago and have gone to the cafeteria for some Coke. If you want to leave…"

"No rush." He settled into a chair across from her "Is she doing okay?"

"She did break her ankle." Beth bit her lower lip. "I just feel so bad for her. If I hadn't been there, she could've waited a long time for some customer to come in and see her on the floor. And if she'd been up on the bookshelf ladder…" Beth shuddered.

"But that didn't happen. She'll probably be out of here in no time flat, and back to work as usual."

"Not if her dad as anything to say about it. He wants her and the boys to come stay at his place for a while so he can take care of her, because her husband travels for a week at a time."

"She's lucky to have family close by."

Beth looked down at her folded hands. "I've been praying there's nothing more serious going on. The doctors seem to be concerned about the heart rate. If she loses her baby…" Her voice broke. "Oh, Dev. I'll feel so *responsible*. The thought of putting anyone else through that…"

She bowed her head lower, and now her slender shoulders were shaking. Was she *crying?*

Feeling way out of his element, he clasped his hands in front of him and shifted in his chair. "I don't know much about this. But surely one of these little critters can handle a few bumps along the way. It has to be the most natural thing in the world, having a baby."

She didn't answer.

He scooted his chair a couple feet closer. "You ought to see the terrible conditions in the remote areas of the Middle East. No medical care. Poor sanitation. And yet there seem to be babies everywhere…doing just fine. Your friend is receiving the best medical care, so she should be perfectly—"

"I think you'd better stop. This is not an easy topic for me."

Wisps of flyaway chestnut hair hung about her face like a veil, but now he saw the teardrops glistening on her hands, and realization dawned.

They'd married so young, well before any thought

of taking on such a grown-up role…and as time passed he'd skirted the topic whenever it came up, the image of his demanding, critical father shouldering its way into his thoughts, filling him with a frightening sense of inadequacy and fear.

What could he possibly know about being a loving father?

Now he remembered the quiet hurt in Beth's eyes that he'd tried to ignore, the longing way she'd cast glances at the little ones in other women's arms. Guilt washed through him. Had he selfishly denied her something she'd wanted more than anything?

"I'm sorry," he whispered, leaning forward to cover her hands with his.

She froze, then pulled her hands away and slowly raised her tear-filled eyes to meet his. "Why?"

He struggled to find the right words, at a loss for what to say. "I guess a lot of women your age start thinking about families. Thinking it'll be too late."

"My age." Her voice turned to ice. "I'm only thirty-two."

"I suppose it's hard seeing your friends….well, like Janet. So you need to find the right guy and you can have kids, too." He floundered on, the words already tasting sour on his tongue. The thought of any other man even asking her out hit him like a punch to the solar plexus. "Uh…right?"

"Right. It's all as easy as can be." She bit out each word.

He shifted uneasily in his seat, knowing he'd just

ended up in a dense minefield without a clue about how he'd gotten there, much less how to escape.

He sighed heavily. "Again, I'm sorry. I didn't mean—"

And now another realization struck with the force of a Mack truck.

"You said that the thought of putting anyone else through this upset you. What did you mean by that?"

"It really doesn't matter."

"I think it does." He reached for her hands again, but she jerked them away and folded her arms over her stomach. "Tell me."

She glanced around the empty waiting room and lowered her voice to a harsh whisper. "Why do you think you have a right to know anything at all? Where were you, all of our married life? And when did you ever care?"

He flinched. "I was military."

"There are strong, loving military families, Dev. You used it as an excuse for distancing yourself from me. When you demanded a divorce, it shouldn't have been such a surprise. You'd walked out of my life emotionally a long time before."

A rush of memories crashed through his thoughts. Blood and screams and fellow soldiers dying in his arms. The smell of death, of bodies lying mangled under heaps of concrete.

"What I did, what I had to deal with when I was away, was nothing I could share with you, Beth. Locking that part of my life away took all the energy I had. I was no longer the guy you married…nothing like him at all. I'm still not—if you can even begin to understand what I'm trying to say."

"I understand that you never gave me a chance to try. Or…to even share things important to me. To us." Her voice broke, and she lifted her chin in defiance. "You came home over two years ago, at Christmas."

"I remember."

"We had a great reunion that lasted all of a day before you walled yourself away all over again. Then you announced that you wanted a divorce, packed up and left. Our 'two weeks' together lasted less than three days before you took off. Great present, by the way."

"I did you a favor, Beth."

"Did you?" She pushed out of her chair and walked the length of the room, stopped at the open door to look down the hallway, then came back to stand in front of him, her arms still folded over her midsection. "Or was it your easy way out? Did your mother tell you? Knowing her, she probably found out and didn't waste any time."

"My…*mother?*" He'd been tracking Beth's anger clearly, but now he stared at her. "What does she have to do with anything?"

Beth glared at him. "You unintentionally left me with the most wonderful Christmas present ever that year. I was pregnant, Dev. Joyously, incredulously pregnant. Nearly delirious with happiness, because I'd thought it would never happen."

He stared at her in awe, and despite all the misgivings he'd ever had about having children, he now felt something warm and wonderful curl around his heart. "You *were?*"

"Even though we'd fought, I planned to tell you—I did." Her eyes filled with tears and sorrow. "But then I started spotting. A lot. The doctor thought I would miscarry. I somehow made it to six months, then seven... though by then, the doc knew there was trouble of another kind."

"I'm so sorry, Beth."

Her eyes were fixed on some faraway point. "They thought I could go longer, and then they'd do a C-section. But I was home one night. Alone. And the blood—" Her eyes squeezed tight. "It came and it came, and even after the ambulance arrived, it wouldn't stop."

He wanted to take her into his arms and console her. To reassure her that there would be other babies in her life someday. But when he moved closer, she stepped back abruptly.

"There'll be another time in your life, honey. Surely—"

"That's another easy way out," she said flatly. "Platitudes and empty promises. But no, there won't be another time. I nearly died in surgery. I lost my little girl. And I'll never be able to have another baby, ever, because of what they had to do to save my life."

Dev suddenly felt sick to his stomach. She'd nearly died because of him—nearly bled to death. And yet he'd already walked out on their marriage, and never knew. "I...I don't know what to say."

"Good, because I'm not quite done." Her sad, quiet smile held no warmth. "I mourned for my baby for a year…and there wasn't a day when I didn't cry over her. I can't even begin to describe the crushing sense of loss, or how I felt during the darkest days of those first six months. Three months after she died, I received an envelope in the mail. Not a condolence card that time. It was my divorce papers."

"The lawyers…"

She waved a dismissive hand. "I'm sure they had no idea. They were just following orders."

He'd never wanted anything more in his life than a chance to enfold her in his arms right now. To comfort her…and himself. But from her stiff posture he also knew she wouldn't accept it. "I don't know what to say, what to do…how I can make any of this better."

"You can't. It's been sixteen months now, and my Lord and I have worked it out after a lot of prayer. How you handle it is up to you…if you care."

"Care?"

She lifted a shoulder. "You were always pretty adamant about not wanting to start a family. So where your emotions are in this, I couldn't guess." She started for the door, then turned back. "For the record, I wasn't ever planning to tell you. My mom was the one who has always insisted that you have the right to know. But as far as I'm concerned, the subject is now closed."

Chapter Ten

A few minutes after Janet's family returned to the waiting room, an intern appeared at the waiting room door.

"Good news," he said with a wide smile. "Every last test looks great, and she can be released as soon as we get her discharge papers done. Baby looks fine."

Beth hugged Janet's father and sons. "Take good care of her, boys. And tell her not to worry about coming into the bookstore. I've got everything covered."

Out in the parking lot, Beth debated about walking home, but Dev stood at the side of his Jeep, holding the passenger side open for her. With a sigh, she climbed in.

"What are you going to do?" he asked as he slid behind the wheel. "Since Janet won't be back for a while?"

"Believe me, that's the least of my worries."

"Do you have anyone in mind?"

"I already offered some part-time hours to Elana, and she agreed. I'll see if she wants to start a little earlier.

She could bring Cody along and let him read books or do homework while she works, and she'd have a chance to save more money. Perfect all the way around."

"If I were a betting man, I wouldn't give you very good odds on her showing up when the time comes."

"I understand why she feels more secure working at the motel. It's out-of-the-way, it's quiet there during the day, there's less chance of being seen. But this would be a good first step for her—a chance to get used to being out in public more."

"Maybe so. I just hope there aren't any deeper reasons for her being scared."

They fell silent on the way to the bookstore. When Dev pulled to a stop at the curb, he turned to face her. "I still don't know what to say. I am so sorry about everything that happened to you. And now I feel this... this big empty place in my chest. Like something huge is missing."

"Welcome to my world, as they say. But I was serious, back there in the waiting room. I didn't tell you for sympathy or to punish you by trying to make you feel guilty. I guess I finally agreed with my mother—that you had a right to know. This won't affect our friendship in any way, I promise. But I don't want to talk about it again."

The idea had seemed perfect.

Elana had agreed.

But when Beth stopped at Sloane House the following afternoon to talk to her about the job at the bookstore, she backed away, twisting her fingers together. "I can't," she whispered. "I—I just can't."

"But the motel only offers minimum wage, and they don't give you enough hours each week. Remember when we talked earlier? It means extra money for your school and a chance to save for an apartment." Beth waved her toward a chair. "Let's sit and talk about it. Okay?"

Elana dutifully sat on the cranberry velvet chair, her gaze flitting around the ornate Victorian decor of the front parlor.

"It would also mean less physical work. You could even keep your old job, if you wanted to. And when Janet comes back to work, I'll still have some hours for you."

"There are other people in this town needing a job. Maybe they would be better for you."

Beth leaned forward, willing the woman to at least make eye contact, but now Elana dropped her attention to her lap.

"Yes, I could advertise, or I could offer the hours to a friend in my book club who has always wanted to work at my store, and I would offer them the same wage I'm offering you. But this is a chance for you to earn more per hour, and get some experience in a retail setting. It will also help you pay for your business classes. And once you're done with them, you'll be ever so much more desirable to an employer. The upscale resorts and business around here would fight over the chance to hire a bright, skilled bilingual woman like you."

"I *know* it would be a good change. But..."

"You have a right to a happy life, Elana, and so does your son. One where you don't need to look over your shoulder in fear."

Elana's eyes glistened with sudden tears. "You don't know what it was like. I was so scared, always. Twice I called nine-one-one, but Roberto would hire his fine lawyers, and then he would be free again. And again we would have to run."

"But that's over. He's where he can't hurt you anymore."

"Yes." Elana wrapped her arms around her stomach. "But what if someone else tries to do the same?"

"It isn't common behavior, Elana. It's against the law. You can get a restraining order or have that person arrested. Dev says he'll be moving to the cottage behind Sloane House soon, and he's been in the Marines for years. If anyone can protect you, he can. Believe me."

She offered a bleak smile. "I would like to."

"Whether or not you decide to work at the store, that's up to you. Either way, I promise you that we'll do our best to help you."

"I...will think about it."

But from the way Elana fled the room, Beth doubted that she'd give it a second thought.

"Wow," Cody whispered. "This is *scary*."

Dev smothered a laugh. "Thanks. And to think it's gonna be my new home."

"You got spiderwebs *everywhere*. And," he marveled, "I'll bet there's even *rats!*"

The boy had slipped out of the boardinghouse as soon

as Dev pulled into a parking place off the alley. He'd
watched from a safe distance at first, then had edged
closer, his caution evident. It had taken him a good ten
minutes to finally gather the courage to reach Dev's
side.

But once there, like most kids, he'd been in awe over
the potential for the scary creatures that might slither,
crawl or fly out of the cottage when the contents were
disturbed.

"Sounds like a great selling point to me. Spiders,
rats—maybe even bats."

At the sound of Beth's voice, Dev turned in surprise.
"I didn't expect to see you here today."

"Why not?" She strolled across the lawn to join them,
no trace of her emotional revelations in her expression
or voice. "I was driving past and saw you two out here.
Thought I'd offer to pitch in." She peered through one
of the dusty windows and whistled. "I know you didn't
want help when I offered before, but try to tell me *now*
that you don't want it. I dare you."

He hesitated.

She turned back to face them. "Cody, you and Dev
can be the spider wranglers, okay?"

Cody looked at Beth uncertainly, and she smiled back
at him. "I ran into Frank and Carl out front, and they're
on their way out here, too. They said they can start
taking off the screens so we can wash the windows."

Beth's smile was for Cody, but it still warmed places
in Dev's heart that had been empty for a long, long
time...though dwelling on those kinds of feelings would
be dangerous. After what she'd been through, there was

no way she'd ever entertain any romantic interest in him again, and he would do well to remember it.

He shook off his wayward thoughts. "Those two old guys don't have to do that. We're supposed to be helping them, not the other way around."

She touched his arm lightly, her eyes taking on a wicked gleam. "Well, they're gathering supplies right now, and they look pretty determined. Go ahead and tell them that they're too old to be doing something like that. I'd like to see a big, tough marine take on Carl and live to tell about it."

Carl and Frank emerged from the back door of the house with steaming buckets of sudsy water, and strode across the lawn to the cottage. With a nod at Dev, Frank disappeared inside the cottage while Carl waited outside a window for his friend to release the latch.

A faint wash of pink infused Beth's cheeks and she pulled her hand away from Dev's arm, as if she'd just realized that she'd been too familiar. "I guess I'd better get busy. Where should I start?"

"Anywhere, I guess."

She walked inside the front door, with Cody and Dev at her heels. "Just look at that lovely stone fireplace and these nice hardwood floors. With a good scrubbing and fresh paint, it's going to be charming." She turned slowly, surveying the room. "But that can't start until everything is out of here. Can you believe all this stuff in here?"

A collection of old lawn mowers, garden equipment and musty furniture filled every inch of floor space; and everything was covered with thick dust and grime.

Through the archway leading into the small kitchen, he could see buckets of old motor oil and dented gas cans that emitted a pungent odor.

Dev wrenched a rusted garden tiller through the living room and lugged it outside to the curb, then returned for an old-fashioned mower and coils of garden hose.

Beth's arm brushed his as she moved past with an armload of rakes and shovels. "Oops, sorry."

She stumbled, caught herself and continued on. Did she feel it too? These flashes from their shared past, when they'd been so aware of each other?

Probably not. She'd made her feelings about him *more* than clear when she'd told him about losing a baby.

On their third trip to the kitchen, a breeze fluttered through the shredded gauze curtains still hanging in the windows. Beth braced a hand on the blistered kitchen countertop and sneezed.

Reva appeared at the doorway. "Bless you."

"Thanks." Beth looked up at her and smiled. "Did you need something?"

"Not at all. Elana is working at the motel this morning, but we all decided we should pitch in." She glanced around the kitchen. "I think I'll go change clothes and bring out a bucket of soap and hot water. I can start cleaning the cabinets as soon as these counters are clear."

"That's a nice surprise," Beth said after Reva disappeared. "The way things are going, we might be able to start painting tomorrow afternoon and get the place furnished by Monday."

He looked at the pile of damaged chairs piled on a

three-legged table leaning against the wall at the far end of the kitchen. "Believe me. There isn't any usable furniture left."

"I'll bet there's extra furniture in the main house, though. In the attic, if nothing else."

"Probably a pink flowered couch, or orange and avocado curtains from the seventies."

She flashed a brief smile. "Just your style."

"I think I'd rather pitch a tent."

"I'm sure you would." She tilted her head and studied him. "By the way, I think Elana is finally considering the job at the bookstore."

"Good for her."

"We sat down and figured out her finances and her schedule, and she should be able to start spring semester classes in January. She'll surely qualify for financial aid—probably even grants and scholarships that she doesn't have to repay. Depending on what happens with that, she wants to find an apartment of her own so she can walk to school and both jobs."

Beth pushed open a door and blindly patted the inner wall until she flipped on a light switch. The single bedroom was packed with a jumble of furniture, with a stained mattress leaning against the far wall. "There you go, Dev." she teased. "You've got a bedroom set in here."

He felt himself sinking, mesmerized by her pretty gray eyes, her silvery laugh. The mistakes of the past had dissolved into nothing, and his focus was narrowed to only her.

"It's not too late," she added.

It's not too late.

She meant it wasn't too late to save these furnishings from going to the growing pile outside, but her words jerked him back to the present.

It *was* too late, no matter what kind of persistent and unwanted attraction he still felt for her. He knew it. Her own mother knew it. And Beth probably hadn't given it a second thought, because she'd already written him out of her life…and given what she'd been through, it was no wonder.

He cleared his throat. "Like I said, a tent is sounding better all the time. But I guess I'd better get back to work."

Twenty minutes later, a car pulled up and three women dressed in faded jeans and old T-shirts piled out. When they headed straight for the cottage, he stared at them in surprise until the one with silver hair veered off to where he was loading junk into a rental trailer.

It took a moment for Dev to place her, given her casual clothes. "Olivia?"

"Ready for duty."

"You're kidding."

"Hannah is still out of town, but the rest of us figured we ought to help out for a few hours. We can't let Beth have all the fun." She fished a business card from the back pocket of her jeans. "And while I'm here, Frank asked me to give you this."

He studied the familiar logo of an outfitter with stores throughout the Upper Midwest. "Great store."

"I totally agree. It belongs to my brother."

"The whole *chain?*"

She shrugged. "He started small, without having the right connections, and struggled for years. If you have questions about suppliers, stock, advertising—anything, just give him a shout. He likes helping newcomers, so I'll let him know that you'll be calling."

"This is wonderful. Thanks."

A smile touched her lips. "He owes me, so I know he'll be very happy to help you. How is it going otherwise? Have you made any progress?"

"I've been sketching plans for displays and shelving, and for the overall floor plan." Dev grinned. "And I stopped at the lumberyard for some materials yesterday morning. The assistant manager helped me place an order for almost everything I need."

"Frank says you're aiming for an open house during the Fall Harvest Festival."

Dev nodded. "He had some great ideas for how I can take advantage of all the foot traffic in town that weekend. Just a half-dozen merchandise shelving units and some posters on the walls will be enough to get the point across. There isn't enough time to do much more right now."

"Good luck. I know Frank thinks you've got a great opportunity there, and he's really looking forward to helping you out."

At eight o'clock that evening, Beth blew the flyaway strands of hair out of her eyes and looked around at the amazing transformation.

The refuse had filled a rented trailer parked outside,

and also formed several towering heaps waiting to be hauled away.

The boardinghouse tenants and her book club had helped Dev and Beth scour every inch of the walls and floors until the place sparkled.

And once it dried, they'd repainted the living room with soft taupe, the bedroom in an inviting shade of silvery aspen, and the kitchen a pale, buttery yellow.

The hardwood floors needed refinishing, but a good buffing tomorrow would bring out the rich amber and gold shades of the oak.

Keeley tamped the lid onto the last gallon of paint. "Wow. Remind me to call you guys when I start fixing up *my* house. You're amazing!"

"This didn't take long at all," Olivia agreed. She glanced at her watch. "And now, I have to run. Anyone want a ride home?"

"I would," Sophie said, peeling off her rubber gloves. "I planned to walk home, but it's getting late and I'm beat."

Keeley nodded. "Me, too."

Beth hugged each of her friends as they headed for the door. "You guys are the greatest. Thanks so much."

As soon as they were gone, she flopped down on the only usable chair in the cottage and closed her eyes. "What a job."

"It wouldn't have gotten done if not for you."

"And all of the others who helped," she said drily. "Don't forget about them."

"But you got them to come. I would still be looking

at five tons of garbage in here and thinking it was a lost cause."

"Don't forget that you have to vacate the premises tomorrow afternoon, while we get the place set up."

"That thought is just plain terrifying."

"Ruffles, lace and chintz, all the way. Count on it."

She smiled to herself as she sorted through her memories of the day...especially the way Frank had tentatively flirted with Reva while she worked on the kitchen cupboards, insisting that she needed help.

She'd staunchly refused, though there'd been a bit of pink in her cheeks afterward, so maybe she wasn't entirely immune to his old-fashioned courtly charm.

Cody and Elana had come by midafternoon, and the way the boy had watched Dev's every move had been so sweet.

"It was good of you to let Cody help with the painting. He was very proud of himself."

"He's a good kid."

"And he's had a lot of tough breaks. I'm glad he could spend some time with you." *You would have made a good father,* she added silently, but she didn't say the words aloud.

Some things were better left unsaid.

Chapter Eleven

Beth paced through her store fluffing pillows on the sofas and rockers and tweaking the book displays.

The tantalizing aroma from a fresh pot of crème brûlée decaf wafted in the air, along with the fragrance of still-warm shortbread cookies she'd baked and dipped in melted Belgian milk chocolate just a few minutes ago.

She paused in the center of the store and spun slowly on her heel, taking in the inviting baskets of ivy and fern hanging in the windows and the colorful afghans draped just so across the backs of the sofas.

Perfect. Just as quaint and inviting as she'd dreamed of, during those long months of feeling lost and alone after her divorce.

With the good friends who would be showing up any minute for their Saturday morning book club, a business she loved, and the warm fellowship and faith she shared with the members at the Aspen Creek Community Church, there was nothing else she needed to make her life complete.

An inner voice whispered Dev's name, but she ignored it. Past mistakes had brought painful lessons that she would not be repeating.

The bells over the front door tinkled.

"Ah…" Olivia stepped inside and took a deep breath as she slipped off her cropped leather jacket. "Now *this* is why we always want our book club to meet right here. What on earth smells so fabulous?"

"Cookies. Coffee. Keeley's bringing the healthy treat this time. A fresh fruit platter, I think."

"You should invite your mother to join us. She's been here over a week and I haven't seen her at all in town."

Beth switched on a stained glass floor lamp by the section on home decorating. "She and I have lunch and go sightseeing together. Otherwise she spends a lot of time resting."

"Is she all right?" Olivia headed for the antique library table, where Beth had set up a fall bouquet and refreshments on her favorite autumn leaves tablecloth. She poured herself a cup of coffee and picked up a cookie, then leaned a slim hip against the table and dunked an edge of the cookie in the steaming brew. "The Maura I remember would be gadding about from dawn to dusk."

"I know. She doesn't seem quite like herself these days. One minute she'll be as breezy as ever, but then she'll seem really pensive…like something is bothering her. She just brushes off my questions when I ask, though."

"If she's the Maura I remember, she'll speak her mind

when she's ready," Olivia said with a smile. "No holds barred."

"That would be Mom," Beth admitted. "She usually doesn't keep you guessing about what she thinks."

"How has it gone with Dev and her?"

"They haven't run into each other much, far as I know. Or if they have, no one's talking and the town is still standing, so it must have gone all right."

"I had a nice chat with him when we came to work on the cottage. And once before, when he was at the Walker Building."

"You did?" Surprised, Beth looked up from pouring herself a cup of coffee, trying to imagine Dev chatting at length with anyone.

He'd become so distant over the years…an intense, guarded warrior who appeared edgy just setting foot in this pretty little postcard of a town that had to be worlds away from the life he led as a marine.

Olivia sipped her coffee. "I have to admit that I'm impressed. With him *and* his plans."

"I know his shoulder injury has to bother him, but he works night and day on that building anyway."

"Frank tells me it's going to be quite a place when he's done. I gave Dev my brother's number so he could talk to someone else in the business." Olivia turned back to the table to scoop a teaspoonful of sugar into her coffee. "He seems like a complex guy. To just look at him, you'd think he's got his life under perfect control."

"If he doesn't, he isn't one to discuss it."

Olivia tipped her head in agreement. "But words unsaid can be just as strong. When I told him how I was proud of him for his military service, he seemed genuinely surprised, as if he couldn't even fathom receiving praise."

"His parents hated that he went into the service. They expected him to be a physician or a lawyer, and drummed it into him from early grade school. When he enlisted, they were outraged. They let him know how much of a disappointment he was. And Vivian never missed a chance to tell him about her friends' children who made the 'right' choices."

"I thought I remembered something like that. I wasn't in her social circle back in those days, of course. Viv was a generation older than me. But gossip in a small town never dies." Olivia frowned. "From the very beginning, she should have been proud and supportive. I rather enjoyed telling him about her change of heart before she died, in case she hadn't found the spine to do it herself. He was *really* surprised at that, so I guess she didn't."

There'd been so much bitterness between his parents and Dev that Beth knew Olivia's description of his reaction was no exaggeration. "What did he say?"

"Nothing. His expression said it all." Olivia tilted her head and studied Beth over the rim of her steaming cup of coffee. "How are you and he getting along? Any nice quiet dinners just to catch up with each other?"

"Hardly. I think we may have progressed from 'painfully awkward' to just awkward. I don't think either of us wants to dredge up the past."

"I'd guess he doesn't confide in many people. He doesn't even talk to you?"

"The few times I've seen him around town when he's

been back, we've barely spoken. There's no animosity. There's just…nothing, as if he has no emotion at all."

"There you would be wrong."

Beth blinked. "You two must have had quite a conversation."

"It wasn't just his words. I think he's really struggling with something, and he could use a friend. Frank Ferguson says the same thing."

"Frank?"

"He and I use to teach together…ages ago. I saw him in the post office yesterday, and he mentioned being really sorry that he startled Devlin on Thursday morning. To quote Frank, 'It was like the poor boy had one of those war flashbacks, or something.'"

"Post-traumatic stress disorder?"

"It would make sense, given what he does for a living. Maybe he needs to get help. Or maybe he just needs someone to talk to. Of all people, you'd be the one who knows him best."

"Not anymore." Beth swirled the coffee in her cup and stared at the dark liquid, trying to dispel the sudden, graphic images of the horrors he'd probably faced. How could anyone ever get over something like that? "And I'd be the last one he'd consider."

Through the front windows, she caught a glimpse of Keeley and Sophie crossing the street together toward the store, walking arm in arm. Relieved at the distraction, she waved to them through the window.

Olivia shook her head in disbelief. She touched Beth's arm and lowered her voice as the other women came in the door. "Don't forget what I said about Dev, honey, because I think that man is really hurting inside."

"I don't—"

"At least try. And say a few prayers for him, too. I'll sure keep him in mine."

At ten o'clock, the antique grandfather clock by the front door started its rich, melodious chime and a customer knocked on the locked door of the store.

Beth went to unlock the door and flip the window sign to Open, then returned to the circle of chairs in the back.

"We didn't get very far with our book discussion," Sophie said ruefully. "And it was my fault, this time."

Keeley and Olivia both enveloped her in a group hug, then Hannah and Beth took their turn.

"Anytime you're having a bad day, you need to call one of us," Keeley said, reaching out to grasp both of Sophie's pale, delicate hands. "I just can't imagine how hard it is to lose a husband. Actually, I can't imagine what's it's like to *have* one, but that's another story."

"Usually, it was pretty nice." Sophie smiled, though her eyes were still damp and her voice wobbled. "I didn't realize our anniversary would hit me so hard this year."

"How is Eli doing? Does he still talk about his dad a lot?"

"He does, almost every day. But that's good for both of us, really. No one at the restaurant or my school even brings it up anymore. I suppose they all think we've had enough time to mourn."

"But they're wrong," Olivia said flatly. "They just haven't been through such a big loss themselves, bless their hearts."

Sophie nodded. "And now, with Eli getting older, he misses having a dad all the more when he sees other dads at school activities and Cub Scouts. I'm so torn—he needs a dad. But I just can't imagine falling in love again. I tried dating again once, and it was a total disaster. Remember Allan?"

Keeley smiled. "Now, you'll have to admit that he was an unusual case. How often are you going to run into someone who was an ex-con?"

Sophie's mouth trembled, then she broke into helpless laughter. "And I didn't have a clue—even when he had those 'coffee meetings with his uncle,' who turned out to be his parole officer. How naive can anyone be?"

"Maybe when you get done with school, and have some time for yourself, you'll find the perfect guy," Olivia said. "Give yourself a break, dear. Things will happen when the time is right."

A stout, middle-aged man walked in from the street, smiling as he passed the members of the book club standing near the door. He continued to the back, and wandered through the bookshelves and displays as the women said their farewells.

His face, with its folds of flesh, made him look nearly identical to the bulldog gracing the cover of this month's *Dog Lover* magazine, displayed not ten feet away from him.

"Duty calls," Beth whispered, hiding a grin. She

turned away from her friends and went to the counter. "How can I help you?"

His benign smile wreathed his eyes in wrinkles. "I'm from out of town, and just wanted to stop by to look around. Nice store."

"Are you looking for anything in particular?"

"Browsing. Is there more upstairs?"

"That's an apartment."

His expression brightened. "Available?"

"No—I live there."

"Long-term? Or might it become available sometime?"

"Long-term."

"Well, I'll bet it's just as charming as your store." He glanced around. "Are there books downstairs, as well?"

"Just storage."

He nodded in obvious satisfaction. "Beautiful old building. Beautiful. I like the old-fashioned bay windows facing the street, and how you've decorated them in such a quaint, appealing way. I'm sure this store draws plenty of tourists down to Hawthorne."

He seemed more interested in the building than the books, but Aspen Creek did draw a lot of people who came to soak up the Victorian flavor of the town and prowl its dozens of antiques shops.

He strolled through the store again, eyeing the crown moldings and pressed tin ceilings, a smile curving his thick lips. "I haven't been inside until now. It used to be a dentist's office, you know. And before that, a milliner's shop. Beautiful views of Aspen Creek and the bluffs, out back."

She eyed him closely. "How did you know that?"

He ducked his head modestly. "Research. And I toured the other buildings along this part of Hawthorne Avenue earlier this morning."

"Why?"

He took a business card from his suit jacket pocket and handed it to her. "I'm here this weekend from St. Paul to check out a few things about the Sloane property."

She stared at the card. "You're Stan Murdock?"

"That's right—Devlin Sloane's uncle." The man smiled beneficently, though his inquisitive gaze continued to roam the store. "He's a fine, fine boy. Is he around, by any chance? Might I be able to see the rest of the building?"

"Devlin doesn't work here. And the basement is just that—stone walls, rather damp, and only used for storage."

"I'll bet the upstairs is positively charming."

"It is."

"Would you mind letting me see it? I so love these quaint old buildings."

He was fishing for permission, but the thought of him snooping through her things up there made Beth's skin crawl. "No. I'm sorry, but there isn't really anything up there for you to see. Nor will there be."

"I was married to Vivian's sister, and I'm named in the will. Are you aware of that?"

"Yes, but—"

"Look, I never understood it, but Vivian had her fun trying to help charity cases. If those people weren't able to get on their feet before she took them in, it's unlikely that any of them can do it now. They are just marking time, enjoying cheap rent."

"I disagree."

"Because you still think you can hang on to this building. But face the facts—you're simply delaying the inevitable," he said gently. "Those people are enjoying themselves at your expense, because they'll still be sitting in that boardinghouse when the deadline is long past....and they won't even care."

"I don't agree."

"But it isn't realistic to assume they'll *ever* be able to find 'careers.' You could save yourself a lot of trouble by relinquishing your rights and walking away."

Stunned, she stared at him. Was the man *crazy?* "I think you need to talk to Devlin."

"I'm heading that way next. With luck, he'll have enough business sense to see that I'm offering both of you a chance to escape the impossible stipulations of his mother's will, *and* come out of the deal with some good money."

Stan's smile had seemed oddly familiar, and now she realized that he reminded her of a smug, self-satisfied cat. "Good 'business sense' would mean turning boarders out onto the street?"

"That's where they'll be when they're still jobless at the end of the six months. And that's what welfare is for." He lifted a shoulder. "I'm just trying to make it easier and more expedient for everyone. You surely don't have time for this nonsense, and I know Devlin wants to get back to the military. I'll even make it worth your while financially, because I have some planning deadlines I want to meet before the first of the year."

"You can't be serious."

His gaze hardened. "I never say anything I don't mean."

"Interesting, because I'm sure you just said that you love 'quaint old buildings' a moment ago."

"I may enjoy touring them, but eventually they become a financial liability. Heating, upkeep, maximum return per square foot—it all has to be considered."

"Well, I say what I mean, too, and I gave my word to Dev and the lawyer, Mr. Murdock. I believe Vivian wanted Dev and I to help the people living in the boardinghouse, not walk away because it would be more convenient."

Again he smiled, but now she saw what lay beneath his gentle facade—a shrewd, hard-nosed businessman who was accustomed to getting his own way. "It sounds like easy math to me. I can offer you ten grand to walk. But if you stay the whole six months and fail to launch every last one of those has-beens, you'll lose the building anyway. Isn't it better to have a guaranteed check in your hand instead of desperately hoping that each one of the boarders can make the grade?"

His arrogance grated against nerves she didn't even know she had. "I don't want to discuss this any further."

"Don't make an enemy of me, darlin'." He narrowed his pale blue eyes on hers. "I'll go talk to Devlin, but in the meantime, you need to think hard about my offer. Because I can guarantee you'll fail to meet the conditions of the will, and then the whole ball game will be mine—*without* having to give the two of you a single dime."

He turned on his heel and walked out, closing the door quietly behind him.

Beth sank against the counter, her knees weak and her pulse racing, thankful that the book club members had left before Stan started talking. But what if he caught Dev at the wrong moment and played his cards just right? Surely Dev wouldn't fall for it.

She hoped.

"Ms. Carrigan?"

The quiet, lightly accented voice came out of nowhere. Beth jerked way from the counter and stumbled back a step.

"I am so sorry," Elana said, a hand at her mouth. "I thought you saw me come in."

Beth could only hope the woman hadn't heard Stan's harsh words. "Can I help you?"

"That man. He said everyone at Sloane House was a failure. No good."

"He is a very *rude* man. And he was wrong."

"I have been thinking about what you said. About the job." Her chin lifted, and her eyes sparkled with defiance. "I am tired of hiding in the shadows. That's why I came."

"You're willing to work here? Really?"

"Now, more than ever. It will give me more money for school, and bigger chances, just as you said. That man who was here thinks I am a failure, but I am going to prove him wrong."

Chapter Twelve

Beth hugged her mother tight. For all of her worries beforehand, the visit had flown by, and they'd reconnected over lattes and treasure hunts through the local consignment stores when Beth had an afternoon free.

"I'm sorry you have to leave," Beth whispered, giving her mother another hug. "Can you come back at Christmastime?"

"I'll try, if only for a couple days. I'll start checking on flights when I get home." Again, a weary look crossed Maura's expression...one of many over the past few weeks, yet she'd refused to say anything about what might be wrong. "The road trip would just be too hard in the winter."

"Please, I need to know. Is something wrong? I've been worrying about you since you arrived."

Maura stepped back and adjusted the colorful scarf around her neck. "Nothing of importance. Worries over my gallery, of course. It's hard to be away, especially through the busy fall season."

Beth rested a hand on her forearm in silent appeal. Maura stilled, then her shoulders sagged.

"I...had a bit of a scare, before I left home. Some lab tests that didn't look quite right, plus an inconclusive CT scan, so they did a biopsy." She smiled wearily. "All this time, I've been waiting for the results, and I finally called this morning. Turns out that the clinic sent the report to my home address, and never thought to call my cell phone. I'd been thinking that this might be my last trip here, and that I needed to settle a lot of things in my life, but I've been worried over nothing."

Relief flooded through Beth as she stepped forward to give her mother another fierce hug. "Oh, Mom."

"I should have trusted more and worried less." Maura's smile turned rueful. "It's hard trying to fix the world when you fear you might only have a short time. I might have been just a *little* hard on Devlin one day. I haven't seen him lately, but extend my apologies if you happen to see him."

After closing up the bookstore at five, Beth found Dev working on the cottage, the windows and doors open to the crisp October breeze.

"Stan Murdock came to see me."

"What did *he* want?"

"He wants us to give up, since we're going to fail anyway. He offered me ten grand to just walk out on the clause in your mother's will. He...um...said he was coming to talk to you next."

"He knows better." Dev looked down at his clenched

fists and relaxed them, flexing his fingers. "My aunt was a successful stock broker, and when he married her it was all about the money for him. I wonder if he ever really loved her. The last thing I'd want is for him to inherit a square inch of Sloane property."

"So you won't deal with him?"

"Let's just say I'd be surprised if he walked in this door. And if money was promised under the table, I'd want to see it in cash and counted before I'd believe anything. Not that I'd take a penny of it."

"He said there was no way we could ever succeed with the residents at Sloane House. Could he...would he do anything to cause trouble?"

"I don't know him that well. But from what I remember, he wasn't dishonest so much as a guy willing to mow right over anyone who stands in his way. Even as a kid, I couldn't see what my aunt saw in him."

"So he's harmless."

"*No one* is completely harmless." Dev thought a moment. "He's a personable guy, but underneath he's a hard-nosed businessman who goes after what he wants. It was underhanded of him to make that offer. But dangerous? I'd guess he's more hot air than anything else. I hope."

"One other thing. Did you happen to have any...um... awkward conversations with my mother while she was here?"

He laughed at that. "Beth, that would typify every conversation she and I ever had, bar none."

"Well, if there was anything in particular that

transpired during her stay here, she wanted me to tell you that she's very sorry—though I have absolutely no idea what she meant."

Beth started for her car, then Olivia's words came back to her and she returned to the cottage, where she found Dev peeling off the last of the blue painter's masking tape from around the frames of the mullioned windows in the living area. "How are you doing, by the way?"

He looked over his shoulder. "Fine. Why?"

"Just wondering. I know your shoulder must be killing you when you work like this. And everything else… well, it can't be easy."

He wadded up the ball of tape and tossed it into a trash can. "Everything else?"

"Well…with all you did in the Marines."

His eyes narrowed on hers, but at least he didn't stalk away. She'd expected that.

"It must be hard sometimes." Flustered by his silence, she stumbled on. "I mean, thinking about some of the bad things that happened. If you ever need to talk to anyone, I'm here."

His gaze still lasered on hers, and several seconds ticked by before he finally shook his head. "Thanks. But there's no need."

Yes, there is, if Frank and Olivia are right and you're jumping at shadows. What would it be like to be living in a nightmare part of the time—and never know when flashbacks might strike? But she couldn't make him talk, and even if he did, what could she say except to offer comforting words or bland, useless reassurances that things would get better?

Maybe they wouldn't.

Maybe he would never really get over the raw experiences he'd had—experiences she couldn't even imagine.

At the thought of the burden he was carrying in his heart, she wanted to go over to him and put her arms around him to give him comfort and support and...

She imagined herself wrapped in his powerful yet gentle embrace, feeling the beat of his heart when she leaned against his hard, muscled chest.

Feeling protected and loved and warm, the way she had a lifetime ago, before everything went wrong. But there was no point in foolish thoughts.

He had changed, and so had she. And there would be no going back.

Chapter Thirteen

"I can't believe we got this done. I think," Beth said with a grin, "that we three should go on television as a home staging team, because we are *amazing*."

"As long as we can get our mitts on a treasure trove of an attic," Keeley laughed. "The wonderful furniture and those burly football players in the youth group made it possible."

"We sure couldn't have carried it all." Olivia studied the living room of the cottage with admiration. "And that boarder of yours is a treasure, too. How did she ever sew the curtains so fast?"

"Elana must've stayed up all night to do it. I don't think she even had a pattern, which impresses me to no end. I can't even hem straight."

Olivia gave the curtains another long look. "Elana works at the motel, right?"

"Part-time there, and also at my store. She's planning on taking business classes at the community college after that."

"Good for her."

At a light rap on the open front door, they all turned to find Dev there, with Frank at his side. "Is it safe to come in yet?"

Olivia laughed. "I want to fight you for the right to live here, but I don't think all my dogs and cats would fit. So you're safe."

He stepped inside, his dark hair ruffled by the brisk October wind, bringing in the sweet scent of the burning leaf pile Carl was tending in the yard. He studied the heavy oak living room furniture, the brass lamps, and the painting of mallards in flight that now hung over the fireplace.

Beth's traitorous heart kicked in an extra beat when Dev surveyed the room a second time, then grinned at her.

"This is beautiful."

"Take a look at the other rooms, too. We found a great bedroom set in your mother's attic, along with a nice pecan table and set of chairs for the kitchen."

Frank checked out the kitchen cupboards. "Looks like they even set you up with dishes and such. I'll bet that was Reva's doing."

"It was indeed," Keeley called out.

"What?" He leaned out of the kitchen, a hand cupped at his ear.

"Reva took care of all that." Keeley tucked a strand of honey-blond hair behind her ear. "Most of the pieces were stored away in the attic. A few pots and pans were extras from the kitchen."

Beth glanced at her watch. "I've got to run. I left

Elana to cover the bookstore for a couple hours, but I'd better get back."

"Keeley and I need to get going, too." Olivia gave him a quick, grandmotherly hug. "Welcome to your new home, soldier."

Elana smiled shyly when Beth walked into the bookstore. "I sold two books while you were gone. And a magazine."

Beth had known it would be quiet on a Sunday afternoon near the end of the tourist season, and on this particular day, she was grateful for it. "So your first cash register lesson was put to work already."

"You'd better check to make sure I did it right. But I think so."

Cody peeked around the corner of the children's section, then limped up to join his mother. "I watched. She did really good!"

Reaching down to ruffle his thick dark hair, Beth smiled. "I'll bet she did. And I'll bet she was glad to have you here with her on her very first day."

He nodded, his face shining with pride.

"I'll tell you what—I'll show you two how to close up, in case you ever have to do that. And then I'll give you a ride home."

"No, you should not bother...."

But Elana's voice lacked conviction, and her uneasy gaze skated to the front windows. Dusk had already fallen, and the six-block walk would get them home well after dark on a chilly night.

"Of course I will. I wouldn't want to walk after dark, either. Now, about closing up at the end of the day…"

After a lesson on closing down the cash register and how to place a special order for books, Elana helped Beth straighten up the store displays, turn off the assortment of lamps and double-check the back-door lock.

"See, it's all easy, and you've caught on really fast. I hope you'll like working here."

Elana nodded, her brow furrowed. "What about your other clerk—will she be able to work soon?"

"She'll be away at least two months with her broken ankle, but she also found out she has some heart problems and says she doesn't want to work nearly as much, even if she does return. You're welcome to all of her usual hours and more, if you want them." Beth grabbed her car keys and purse from the counter. "Shall we go?"

She let Elana and Cody step outside, then she turned to lock the door. At Elana's sharp gasp, she spun around. "What is it?"

Elana had a tight grip on Cody's shoulders. "I—I thought I saw something…just over there." She tipped her head toward the rear bumper of Beth's car. "I don't see anything now."

Darkness had fallen, but the old-fashioned street lamps cast a gentle glow on the street, and there were security lights shining at the peak of each of the other buildings on the block. Beth's car was the only one in sight, its headlights not more than ten feet from the store entrance.

"I don't see a thing," Beth murmured. "And honestly, I don't remember the last time there was any trouble in this area. Six months, at least. It's a safe place to live."

"But strangers can come here," Elana whispered. "They could come from anywhere, and think this place is...is...an easy mark, *sí?*"

"I've never felt afraid in Aspen Creek. A lot of people leave their doors unlocked. People trust each other here, Elana." Beth offered an encouraging smile. "The sheriff and his lone deputy might be straight out of Mayberry, but they don't have much to deal with. I've even heard one of the deputies complain that an occasional shoplifter was the most excitement they saw all year."

Elana cast another uneasy look over her shoulder.

"And now, in the middle of October and on a Sunday night, there ought to be very few tourists still around, if any." Beth reached for her cell phone and held it aloft. "Don't worry, though—I've got my phone, and just pressing the 9 will call 911. But I've never had to use it here, believe me."

She circled her car, checked the backseat, then once again surveyed the empty street. "All clear. I'm sure of it."

A cat appeared far down the sidewalk, its tail held high as it marched in the opposite direction. With a meow he vaulted over a gate between two buildings and disappeared.

Elana's shoulders sagged with relief. "A cat. Only a silly cat. Right, Cody?"

Despite all reassurance to the contrary, she scurried forward when Beth hit the button on her key ring to unlock the doors, pushed Cody inside, then clambered in after him and hit the door lock on her side.

She was still breathing heavily and muttering under her breath in Spanish when Beth got in and locked her own door.

"There," Beth soothed, seeing the frightened expression in Cody's eyes. She glanced over her shoulder at the empty rear seat, then started the engine. "We're all safe. It was just a cat, after all."

But after she pulled away from the curb and started down the block, she flicked a glance at the empty street in the rearview mirror.

It wasn't hard to see how Elana had become so wary. Just being with her and sensing her fear had made Beth's own heart rate escalate for a few beats.

What would it be like for a woman like Elana, whose bogeyman was real?

Once Elana and her son were safely back at Sloane House, Beth drove home and parked on the street directly in front of the entrance.

The street was still empty and brightly lit…a street she'd lived on for some time now, without ever being afraid. Again her thoughts turned back to Elana and her son—who had obviously picked up on his mother's fears tonight. What had they been through in the past to still affect them so deeply? What was it like to live in such terror?

The wonder of it was that Elana had found the courage to move here alone with her son and go out of the house every day for her job. *I think I see my first mission at Sloane House, God,* she murmured to herself. *But I'm going to need Your guidance. I need to find a way to help that woman or she'll never, ever be free of her past.*

Headlights appeared at the far end of Hawthorne, coming her way. Devlin's Jeep, she realized as the vehicle passed under a streetlight. Grabbing her purse and keys, she stepped out of her car and waved to him as she moved to the entryway leading up to her apartment.

He pulled to a stop behind her vehicle and jumped out. The soft light of the street lamps made his dark hair gleam, and cast intriguing shadows on the planes and angles of his face.

He was still, and always would be, the only man who had ever made her pulse race just with his presence... though the days of wanting to recognize those feelings were long past.

So how long was it going to take for her heart to accept it?

"Am I ever glad you weren't here twenty minutes ago," she called out. "Elana was spooked by every shadow when we came out of the bookstore to take her and Cody home. She probably would have collapsed if she'd seen a car come up the street."

His tense expression softened. "That's where you were? I tried calling the bookstore, but there was no answer. And you didn't answer your cell phone, either."

Surprised, she fished it out of her purse and studied the screen. "Oops. I had the ringer too low to hear when it was in my purse. What's up?"

"I was worried."

"Worried? There's no reason to be." But she could see he was breathing hard and his eyes were dark and dilated, and she knew he was telling the truth. "I think you've gotten overly cautious in your old age."

"You shouldn't be living here, away from a residential area."

"I *love* my home."

"It isn't safe."

"It's fine. The person who needs help is Elana. I think every sound and shadow is enough to stop her heart. How is she going to function independently unless she gains more confidence?"

He frowned and folded his arms across his chest. "Maybe you should stay at Sloane House."

Startled, she stared at him. "You're not serious."

"I mean it. There's a maid's apartment on the third floor that isn't in use. Or there are some sofas on the main floor."

She smiled at him. "I have a security system—not that I expect it will ever earn its keep. If someone breaks in, the police are summoned unless I press a code on the keypad."

"But it's an understaffed department that could be occupied by a fender bender or a cat up a tree. And if you don't have a good security system, an expert can get in anyway."

"I'm not staying at Sloane House. The idea is ridiculous."

He gave a long sigh. "When did you become this stubborn?"

"When did you become such a guardian angel?" she countered. Looking up at him, she realized that all of this was because he cared for her still. And suddenly she had the oddest sensation that he wanted to kiss her. *Where was that coming from?*

He gave her a fierce hug, then stepped away, only to bend down to drop a swift kiss on her mouth. And from the dazed look in his eyes, he was nearly as surprised as she was.

She'd looked up at him wide-eyed and dazed, and he knew his impulsive, possessive kiss had rattled her more than any prospect of an intruder.

He hadn't meant to do it. He didn't have the right. But something about her living out here alone and defenseless had triggered a primitive, protective instinct deep inside him, and it had taken all his willpower to step away before he kissed her again.

"Maybe you'd better go," she whispered.

He dutifully took another step away from her. "I can check out your store and apartment while you wait here," he offered, not quite ready to just climb behind the wheel of his Jeep and drive away.

"If anyone got through those doors while I was gone, the police would already be here. Believe me." She sighed. "But okay. Come up and check things out if it'll make you feel better, but then you'll have to go."

"Of course."

She unlocked the door leading to the upstairs and ushered him on ahead of her. When he reached the upper floor and opened the door, he drew in a slow breath. "This is nice, Beth."

A subdued, stained-glass chandelier hung over the kitchen table, bathing the area in warm golden light.

An inviting, deep plush sofa and love seat in dark cranberry were angled toward a small fireplace, with lush green plants sitting on windowsills and oil paintings of the Rockies adorning the wall space not filled with bookshelves.

The place felt warm, cozy and inviting, unlike the overly feminine touches at Sloane House that made him leery of sitting on fragile chairs.

Here, in Beth's tidy kitchen, the oak cabinets, marble countertops and expanse of windows were probably even more beautiful during the day with sunshine streaming inside and everything so neatly cleared of clutter.

Though taped to the refrigerator was something oddly out of place—a layout for some sort of a building, sketched in detail…with cross-outs and arrows, and notes at all angles.

But that's not your business. Nothing in Beth's personal life is your business anymore.

He jerked his attention back to his mission and took a quick tour through the apartment, then met her at the entryway. "Looks good. But don't forget—I'd be happy to come any time, if you're worried about anything."

She smiled. "I really appreciate your concern. But I'm a big girl now. Not the shy little thing you married all those years ago."

"No, I guess not. About that…"

She shook her head. "Over and done with." She

opened the door to the stairway, hesitated, then turned and brushed a quick kiss against his check. "Thanks, Dev. I appreciate it."

And when she shut the door behind him, she took a piece of his heart with her.

Chapter Fourteen

With Dev's permission, Beth lent his late mother's car to Elana, and insisted that she drive to and from her jobs at the motel and bookstore, and when she took Cody to school.

Dev, bless his heart, had become something of a private guardian, driving past the bookstore after dark, perhaps coming by more times than she even knew. With both the loaner car and his reassuring presence, Elana seemed to gain confidence with every passing day.

In the process of working with the residents of Sloane House, Dev and Beth had both ended up at the house for several casual lunches with whoever happened to be home at the time. There'd been no mention of that kiss or warm embrace, though the memory hung between them like a minefield, and they tiptoed through every encounter, polite and formal and businesslike.

But today, with the town's Fall Harvest Festival in full swing for the entire weekend, there'd be little time for leisurely talks over sandwiches and coffee.

Beth surveyed the bookstore and smiled. "You've been a wonderful help, Elana. I think we're ready, don't you?"

Pumpkin-scented candles on candle warmers were placed strategically high, away from the reach of toddlers and the grade-school finger-dippers who wanted to play with the fragrant, melted wax.

Arrangements of fall leaves and chrysanthemums graced the larger tables and the front counter, where separate bowls of Halloween-decorated cookies and pumpkin-shaped homemade dog biscuits—unfrosted, so there'd be no confusion as to which was which—awaited the crowd of tourists who came to Aspen Creek for the weekend festivities.

Elana leaned over the fall-themed display in the front bay window to look out at the booths lining the streets, and the growing crowd. "It is fortunate to have such a sunny Saturday. It should be a very big day, yes?"

"I hope so. All of us are offering big sales, and the newspaper and radio ads in the Twin Cities should bring traffic our way. I hear the B and B's and motels are all full."

Elana leaned farther on her braced hands, until her nose practically touched the glass. "There is a *very* big crowd in front of Dev's store."

Beth joined her at the window and felt a thrill of excitement over the gathering of people at that end of the block. "It looks like it's quite a hit."

Though only a sampling of the stock had arrived and the display units and shelving weren't completely in, he and Frank had put up colorful posters inside to advertise the type of stock and services that were yet to come.

Four kayaks had come, though, in a brilliant rainbow of colors, and were displayed out in front, just as he'd first envisioned.

"Well," Beth said, taking a deep breath. "It's ten o'clock and time to open the doors. Are you ready?"

Her dark eyes shining, Elana nodded. "I think this will be a day to remember."

When he'd first heard the details of his mother's will, Dev had imagined six long months of responsibility while playing nursemaid to a houseful of faceless old folks who probably needed a higher level of care.

He'd been here a full month, and his perception had changed a hundred-eighty degrees, challenging every single day his original plan to stay emotionally distant until he could finally escape.

Cody had become his shadow.

Frank, with his strong organizational skills, had been teaching Dev about running a business, but in a fatherly, gentle way that was totally the opposite of Dev's own late father.

Even Carl had come over to help with the carpentry on the interior of the store, and he'd worked faster and harder for his money than most men half his age. The others from the boardinghouse had dropped by now and then to help unpack boxes, sweep and dust, or just to offer encouragement.

His houseful of faceless, unwanted responsibility had started to feel like family.

"Hey, son," Frank called out from the front door. "Someone wants to buy a kayak and is asking about accessories."

Dapper as ever in his worn suit, crisp white shirt and tie, Frank had conceded to the theme of the store by exchanging his bomber hat for a fishing cap emblazoned with a giant, thrashing walleye embroidered on the front.

Glancing at the fierce fish on his head, Dev raised a hand in acknowledgment, finished a sales transaction for spandex biker shorts and a new brake assembly for a mountain bike, then locked the register and made his way through the crowd to the front door.

Frank met him at the door and rested a hand on Dev's back as he pointed out the right customer.

"I should have hired extra help today. I had no idea," Dev said, close to Frank's ear.

"If you'd like, I could call Reva. She knows how to handle a cash register."

His eyes sparkled and a note of pride crept into Frank's voice whenever he spoke of the woman who was apparently the love of his life, though she didn't appear to be aware that he even existed. Still, he doggedly treated her with proper, courtly respect at every opportunity.

"Good idea. Thanks." Dev gave him a hearty clap on the shoulder, wishing he could do more to smooth the way for his friend. Maybe…if the store stayed busy, he could hire her part-time, so she and Frank would end up working together…

He snorted at the thought. Of all people on the planet,

he was the last who ought to interfere with anyone else's affairs of the heart. He'd loved Beth Carrigan with all his heart once, and where it had gotten him?

Long nights.

Little interest in anyone else.

Businesses at opposite ends of a block.

And occasional working lunches, when they talked about the people of Sloane House and wondered what to do about them.

But that was life. He searched out the kayak customer and worked his way over there. "Hey, how can I help you?"

And smiled to himself, because it was so ironic that he could make that offer to someone else yet not be able to help himself.

By five o'clock, the crowds had thinned to a trickle. Dev's shoulder was aching, his feet were tired, and Frank looked exhausted.

Reva, who had handled the cash register for hours as well as finding varying sizes and colors of items for customers in the back room, looked as fresh as a pristine, ivory rose, her posture perfect, her black hair and elegant features unruffled.

"I'm going to run across the street and get us all some coffee," Frank announced, his eyes shyly fixed on Reva. "Black with cream and one sugar?"

She inclined her head in a regal nod. "Thank you, Frank."

The woman needed to give him more points for effort, Dev thought as he restocked a display of Swiss

Army knives by the front door and watched Frank head across the sidewalk. Belatedly, he realized he should have given Frank some cash.

Locking the glass display, Dev started out the door. "Frank!"

Frank paused at the curb, then started across the street.

"Frank—wait a minute." Dev started after him, caught behind a family moseying down the sidewalk with a herd of small, sticky children holding balloons that were bobbing crazily in the breeze at adult eye level.

From the corner of his eye he saw a dark sedan pull slowly from the curb at the far end of the block. As it drew closer he caught a glimpse of a teenager driver holding a cell phone at his ear, while juggling a coffee mug and the steering wheel with his other hand.

The balloons bobbled back into Dev's line of vision just as the sedan suddenly swerved and lurched forward.

A sudden premonition sank its talons into his heart. "Frank! Look out!"

Oblivious, Frank kept walking.

Someone screamed. Stragglers in the street scattered, gripping the hands of small children as they threw themselves out of the way.

Startled by the motion more than the noise, Frank spun around and started to run.

But it was too late.

The car caught him broadside. His body tumbled in the air as if in slow motion, then landed with a sickening thud and the sound of fractured bone on the street, a good twenty feet from impact.

People shouted. The scene was a blur of color and movement as the vehicle screeched to a stop, then took off around the next corner on two wheels and rocketed out of sight.

Dev started running. Even as his mind automatically clicked into emergency mode, his heart wrenched with grief for an old man who couldn't possibly sustain injuries from that kind of impact and survive.

And for the first time in years, he started to pray.

"I failed. I could've saved him, but I failed," Dev ground out, his elbows propped on his thighs and his face buried in his hands.

Beth rested a hand on his shoulder blade, wishing he would sit back in his chair and make eye contact. When she'd arrived in the E.R. waiting room he'd been sitting alone, bent over his knees with his fists clenched behind his head. Lost in his own world, he hadn't acknowledged her greeting or her presence for a good twenty minutes.

Whether he was praying or reliving Frank's accident she couldn't guess.

But then he'd straightened up in his chair, and had been berating himself ever since, refusing to listen to reason. His guilt and grief were so palpable that it seemed the whole room was filled with it.

"He's lucky to have a good friend like you, Dev. You can be supportive while he's in the hospital. You can help him once he's released."

"He's *lucky?* Think again. Someone else would've moved faster. Done the right thing."

"You were too far away. He couldn't *hear* you over the noise of the other people."

"As for being a good friend? I have nothing to give him or anyone else. I can't even *relate* to civilian life. Not anymore."

With a sudden flash of clarity, she realized this was not just about the gravely wounded man who'd been in surgery for almost two hours now, facing a battle for his life.

She placed her hand over his and squeezed gently. "You tried to warn him. You tried to get there in time. It wasn't possible for anyone to do better. He's in God's hands now."

"God's hands." Dev's voice was low and bitter. "Where was God whenever I prayed desperately for someone's life? When that hit-and-run driver headed for Frank and accidentally stepped on the gas instead of the brakes? Where was God when that Afghan mother and her two kids—"

He broke off sharply and leaned his head against the wall above his chair, his face pale.

Beth's heart twisted at the depth of pain he felt, far beyond that of any battle wound or surgery, though he'd endured those as well. She let the silence between them lengthen, letting him think. Hoping he might start talking again.

But he stared up at the ceiling as if she weren't there, one minute after another.

"Tell me," she said quietly.

He shot her such a disparaging glance that she felt as if he'd scorched her skin. She was tempted to get up and walk away, but something made her sit still.

"If you think I won't be able to understand what you've been through, you're wrong. It may tear at my heart and I might never forget it, but it's a part of you. I need to know."

He closed his eyes. "We were on a reconnaissance mission in a remote, rugged area outside of Kabul. It's no place you'd want to be. Scorpions, vipers, cobras, and some of the roughest terrain you'll ever see. We came under fire and took position in a bombed-out village— not much more than a pile of rocks. But there was a woman hiding there, with two small kids. She was so young, so scared—you could see it in her eyes, but she'd created a shelter for those little boys, and you could see she was doing the best she could for them. And when we showed up, we brought trouble right to her door."

He sighed heavily and fell silent.

Beth could guess the horrifying outcome. She didn't want to hear the words. But she also knew it was more important for Dev to finish what he was saying than to keep it inside.

"Please—go on."

"When we came under fire again, I urged her to take her children to a building at the rear of the compound. I figured the enemy would have to get past us before she'd be in any danger. But they must have seen me go back there—maybe thought we had a cache of weapons inside. They used a grenade launcher and reduced it to a pile of rubble in minutes." He finally opened his eyes and met Beth's gaze.

"There isn't a day or night when I don't hear those children screaming, and hear their poor mother desperately calling for help. But they were all dead when we got there. And it was because of me."

"Is that where you got hurt?"

He tipped his head in acknowledgment.

From his silence, she knew he hadn't just hidden in a safe place during the bombing. He'd probably risked his life trying to save those civilians' lives, and then nearly lost his own in the process.

It was probably a miracle that he'd survived.

"In war...you aren't responsible for everything that happens. You can't know what the outcome will be, even if you did your best. It wasn't you who launched the grenades."

"But I was praying like crazy when that attack started, yet my decision led those children to their deaths. And I tried to save Frank from being hit, but those desperate prayers didn't help, either. So tell me. Where was God in all of this? Maybe you have a direct line to God, but He sure doesn't listen to me."

She closed her eyes briefly. *God, please give me the right words.*

"Let me tell you what I believe, Dev." She hesitated, expecting he might launch to his feet and walk away, but he didn't move. Was he even listening? "God never promised us that life would be fair. That good people would have perfect lives. Or bad people would face perfect justice here on earth. I believe that men have free will to do good or evil, and if they do something evil, it isn't God's will at all. He loves his children and wants them to have full, abundant lives."

Dev made a noncommittal sound deep in his throat.

"God *does* listen to prayer."

"Right."

"Sometimes, He answers in ways we don't understand, or we don't like, or in His own good time." She dropped her gaze to her hands, trying to search for the right words. "Sometimes, it's a small and perfect answer—one of those little miracles in life. Sometimes, like when my dad died, it isn't that He cures the fatal disease or stops the runaway train or fixes the terrible injury. He brings us peace and comfort and healing."

Dev didn't respond, so she soldiered on. "And sometimes He brings the answers and support we need, through each other. I can't tell you how many 'random' things happened after my dad died—chance meetings or phone calls, the support of strangers—that helped me through those days. I still wish I'd kept a list."

She ventured a look at Dev, hoping to see acceptance and understanding. Instead, he'd leaned back again, his eyes closed, and her heart fell.

But with that came the realization that she'd been right. He already carried a heavy burden of grief and guilt in his heart. Sharing the truth about what happened after he ended their marriage had simply added one more sad chapter in his life among the many.

And nothing could change the past.

A nurse in scrubs appeared at the door, a surgical

mask dangling from her neck. She looked weary, her eyes already telegraphing a message Beth didn't want to hear.

Dev straightened instantly at the sound of her footsteps, his attention riveted on her.

"Are you two here for Mr. Ferguson?"

Dev nodded.

The nurse hesitated. "We can't talk to anyone except family, unless we have a signed release. But the gentleman has nothing on record in either case."

"He was never married, I know that much. Devlin and I manage Sloane House, where Frank lives."

"He works for me," Dev added. "And he's a friend. Can you tell us anything at all?"

"He is in recovery. If he becomes lucid enough to sign the proper releases, then I can tell you more." She jotted down their names, then turned and disappeared down the hall, her shoes squeaking rhythmically on the gleaming tile floors.

"*If* he recovers enough?" Dev's voice was low and raw. "She might as well have said that he won't make it, because that doesn't sound good at all."

"And that, Dev, is why I'm praying."

Chapter Fifteen

"No one caught a license on that car?" Dev stared across Frank's hospital bed at Sheriff Long in disbelief. "There were people everywhere—still in the booths along the street. Pedestrians on the sidewalk. It looked like the car was *parked* before it hit Frank."

The sheriff's bushy red eyebrows drew together. "Several people identified the make and model as a Ford Escort. A witness said he saw a teenager get behind the wheel with some sort of coffee mug. How common is that? No one would've thought anything of it."

"*And* he had a cell phone in his hand."

"It's definitely a hit-and-run, all right. That boy will face serious charges when we find him."

"So what are you doing about it?"

"I've put out an alert for a car and driver of that description with possible fender damage, and the radio and newspaper have run it as well. From all accounts, it was an accident, not intentional—probably a moment of distraction by a cell phone, confusion between the brake and accelerator pedals, coupled with just plain, bad judgment."

"But there will be charges."

"If we find our boy, and the investigation warrants them, yes. But Mr. Ferguson here also failed to hear shouts of warning, so some responsibility is in his court."

"From what I saw—"

"You were stressed, experiencing great anxiety and an adrenaline rush, no doubt, when you saw an elderly friend wander into the path of a car going down the street."

At that, Frank opened his eyes and glared at the sheriff. "I'm not elderly, and I *never* 'wander.' I stride, with great purpose." Shifting slightly in bed, he winced in pain. "Though after this mishap, the doctors say I may not be doing that so well anymore."

Dev rested a hand on Frank's shoulder while he looked the sheriff straight in the eye. "A severe concussion, fractures of his femur and ankle, and internal injuries aren't serious enough?"

The sheriff stiffened. "Like I said, we'll do what we can."

Dev listened to the sheriff's heavy footsteps move down the hall. "Well, what did you think of that example of small-town police work?"

"Guess I should've kicked the bucket, so he'd stand up and take notice."

Dev cracked a smile. "Don't go having second thoughts."

"Definitely not." Frank beamed. "Reva came to visit

first thing this morning. She brought me new hearing aid batteries and read me my greeting cards."

"I thought you'd read them all. You were telling me about some of the messages."

Frank's eyes twinkled. "It sure doesn't hurt to hear them again."

So, at least there was a small silver lining in all of this. Until yesterday, Frank had been in a lot of pain, and in a fog from his meds. Today, he looked the best yet, and he'd even been able to flirt a little with the woman he admired.

"Your secret is safe with me." Dev looked out the window and saw the sheriff wedging his belly behind the wheel of his patrol car. "I wonder if Sheriff Long will follow through with an investigation."

Frank rolled his head against the pillow. "We've had better sheriffs over the years. But so far, this one hasn't absconded with county funds or used his budget to finance a trip to Vegas, so he's better than most." He gave Dev a calculating look. "We could still do better. He'll be up for re-election next year. If you change your mind about the store, you could look into giving him a run for his money."

"Me?" Dev snorted.

"With your military service, why not? Might just be the breath of fresh air we need around here."

Staying in Aspen Creek had never been on his list of possibilities, yet now, he had the beginnings of a new retail venture, and there might even be other opportunities to explore.

He rolled his shoulders, tensing the muscles, testing

his mobility. Pain lanced down his arm like a lightning bolt, sharp enough to make him draw in a quick breath.

It would heal in time, enough for whatever the civilian world held for him. The future no longer looked as grim as it had back at the VA, when his life had changed in the thirty seconds it took for that fresh-faced doctor to give him the bad news.

He thought of Beth and felt a glimmer of hope. Maybe the future wouldn't be so bad after all.

Beth smiled at the residents of Sloane House who were seated at the dining room table, then took an empty seat next to Dev. "Sorry we were slow to schedule our monthly meeting with you all."

"After what happened to Frank, none of us even thought of it," Reva said. "In our spare time, we try to visit him as often as we can."

"It's great that you do," Dev said. "He appreciates everyone's visits very much. The hours must drag, lying in a hospital bed day after day."

Carl nodded. "Any word on when they'll spring him?"

"His doctors are saying that he might be released soon, but he'll be housebound for some time. He'll need visits from a home health aid and physical therapists for a month or two…maybe more."

Elana bit her lower lip. "He will need a first-floor room. I can give him the one Cody and I share. We might be leaving in December or January, so we could take his small room upstairs for a while."

"That soon?" Beth exchanged a startled look with Dev. Elana was so wary about the least shadows—how could she manage alone? "Don't rush things if you don't have to. When we were discussing your future plans earlier, didn't you say you were figuring on late spring?"

"With my jobs at the bookstore and the motel, I will soon be ready to be on my own." She looked down at an envelope laying in front of her on the table cloth. "After Christmas, I will start looking for a small place that will work for Cody and me."

Beth frowned. No matter how she and Elana had juggled the numbers recently, a move into a private apartment was almost impossible, unless...

"Did you hear something from the college?"

Elana's lower lip trembled as she smiled and held the envelop aloft. "I have been accepted into the college, yes. Spring term."

Applause broke out around the table.

"That's wonderful," Reva exclaimed as she rounded the table to give the younger woman a hug.

"I'm so proud of you, Elana," Dev said. "Did you hear anything about your financial aid package?"

"Not yet. But I called. The secretary said I should hear very soon and that everything will be fine. I qualified for several grants, because I am an older person coming back to school. And," she added with a shy smile, "because there was a special scholarship for first generation Latinas. It is from a lady dentist in town."

"Good news," Carl said, a smile softening his usual gruff tone.

Elana stood and picked up her envelope. "I am sorry,

but I need to help Cody with his homework. Excuse me, please."

A hush fell over the group after she left the room, then Reva cleared her throat. "I hope she isn't trying to move out too quickly. She has a lot of responsibility, with Cody to take care of. Here, we watch him for her so she doesn't need to worry about babysitters."

Carl nodded. "I'll miss that little guy if he moves on."

"Dev and I will talk to her," Beth said quietly. "I know we all want her to make the right decision."

"So as far as the rest of you go, how are you doing?" Dev leaned back in his chair.

"I've put in more job applications, but nothing so far. Just because I'm almost fifty-nine with a few little heart problems, they see me coming and imagine the worst," Carl grumbled. "I'd put in twice the work most of those young kids would—no work ethic in any of them, these days."

Beth tapped her pen against her lower lip. "I would've thought that you'd receive long-term disability, since you were hurt on the job."

"The railroad said I can't prove I was, and the pension I get right now isn't enough to live on."

"Did you have a lawyer work on this?"

"With what? I didn't have any money."

"That's going to be my next project, Carl." Beth jotted a note on her tablet. "I'll look into legal assistance options, and see what we can do."

"My former brother-in-law does some pro bono work, but usually for city employees who have been wrongfully fired," Reva said. "I can ask him if he could handle this or would know someone with the right experience."

"Fantastic. Just let me know. Between the two of us, maybe we can come up with something."

After a moment, she looked up. "How about you, Reva? Is there any way we can help you?"

"First, I want to tell everyone how much this place and your friendship have meant to me over the past few months, while I've been trying to decide what to do." Reva pressed her lips together. "As you all know too well, I've had a hard time getting back on my feet since my husband died. His death and the revelation about our financial picture were a blow, to say the least."

Carl scowled, his lined face drooping into bulldog wrinkles. "I'd like to give him what-for."

"But it was my fault, too." She toyed pensively with her pearl necklace. "He never wanted me to 'worry my pretty head' about our finances, but that was a big mistake on my part. No woman should be as ill informed as I was, for so many years. I just never expected…well, that's getting to be an old song, isn't it?"

"Anyone would struggle with the losses you've faced," Beth said. "Seems to me that you've handled everything with a lot of grace."

"And prayer. It's sad to think that I might have been neglecting that part of my life all these years. It took these troubles to remind me that I don't need to only rely on myself."

Dev looked up from the notebook in front of him. A faint, wry smile touched his mouth. "And that helped."

"In subtle ways, and in concrete ways I couldn't have imagined. Like old friends, calling out of the blue to be supportive. Chance meetings, and newspaper articles that I come across that speak to my situation. A growing sense of peace that everything, somehow, will work out. And last night, I got a call from my cousin down in Orlando. We barely exchange Christmas cards and I hadn't talked to her in *years,* yet she thought to call…and this morning, I got an e-mail from an old acquaintance."

"That's nice, but…"

"My cousin said she'd like to talk to me about coming down to manage her clothing boutique. Gerard is in Michigan, and asked if I'd be interested in helping him run his insurance office."

"That's wonderful." Beth smiled at her. "What do you think of those opportunities?"

"Just having options has given me a feeling of hope. I'd still like to stay in this area, if I can. I've been reading the advertisements all along, afraid to try for the jobs that intrigued me the most. Now…what do I have to lose? It won't be so devastating if I'm turned down, because now I have a fallback plan."

Beth thought about her dream for the youth center in the empty building next to the bookstore. If she ever got the program started, it might someday become self-supporting with the right kind of church and community support. Eventually it might need a director with good fundraising and people skills. Someone like Reva, who had been well entrenched in the community all her adult life.

But that day was so far-off that it didn't even bear mentioning.

"I'll bet you'll be surprised at how many opportunities you find. With your social connections, you shouldn't have any trouble at all."

"I'm afraid I might have been a bit...lofty in my day." A faint, sad smile touched Reva's mouth. "The Bible verse is right about 'pride goeth before the fall.'" I imagine some of those old connections might find my financial straits and job search amusing, though that's probably no more than I deserve."

"Or, they might find it impressive that you're choosing to find enjoyment and satisfaction by seeking a career so you can be an independent woman. That would be my view."

"Thanks, dear. You are such a sweetheart." Reva skated a calculating look at Dev. "Though I wonder if everyone is sharp enough to see it."

After adjourning the brief meeting, Dev walked Beth out to her car. "So, what do you think? Are we on track?"

"So far. We *just* need to send our report to the two lawyers at the end of the month, and we'll be set. One month down, five to go." Leaning a hip against the front fender of her car, she nibbled on her lower lip. "It sounds like Reva has some options, now."

"Carl doesn't. He hasn't the strength or stamina to put in a day at the kind of work he's always done...yet I don't think he'll ever be happy unless he can prove himself again."

"But if he doesn't brighten up his attitude, he won't even get to first base at an interview." Beth's mouth twitched. "I'm just imagining trying to get him to role play proper interview techniques. It isn't easy."

Bracing a shoulder against the door frame of the car, Dev laughed. "I can give him a man-to-man talk about attitude, but I think I'll leave the rest up to you."

"Thanks," Beth retorted. "If I survive that, then we also need to talk to Elana. She's one of the most emotionally fragile women I've ever met, and she has a support system here with the other tenants and with us. Why would she want to leave so soon? Even if she gets her scholarships, she could save money for the future by staying here long as she can."

"You're right, though she's also a free woman and can do what she wants."

"But isn't our role to provide whatever help and guidance we can? Not just because of your mom's will, but because it's *important*. I think…"

Sunshine dappled down on them through the canopy of bright maple leaves overhead. A cool breeze kicked up an eddy of fallen leaves that swirled around their feet. A perfect fall day…made all the more perfect because of the chance to stand here and talk to Beth. Just as he had all those years ago when they were teens…before they grew up and life became so complicated.

"Well?" Beth said, eyeing him closely.

He jerked his thoughts back to the present. "Well what?"

"Any news about that hit-and-run driver?"

The topic felt like a splash of ice water. "The sheriff doesn't have a name. He ran various combinations of similar makes, years and models of the car, but no luck so far. He's guessing it might have been a tourist from out of the area—maybe the boy's family was staying at one of the resorts. If the car went back to Minneapolis or Chicago, it would be like hunting for a grain of rice on a beach."

"So isn't that a lead in itself?"

"Not enough for a sheriff's department the size of this one—they have almost no manpower. And—thank heavens—this isn't a vehicular manslaughter case."

Beth shuddered at his words. "I've thanked God more than once about that. Have you heard when Frank will be released?"

"Frank says it depends on his therapy and healing. With his fractured hip, things are going slow."

"Poor guy. I'll bet he hates being confined."

Dev grinned. "Not as much as you might expect, since Reva has been visiting him every day."

"Silver linings?"

"Silver linings," he echoed as Beth waved and walked away, realizing that there'd been plenty of those for him, too.

With every passing day, he felt drawn deeper into life here in Aspen Creek. Closer to the residents of Sloane House, who were all so unique, and so opinionated. He couldn't have been more wrong, when he'd first arrived and assumed they were just a group of old folks in need of care.

Dev headed for the cottage, and he couldn't help but laugh at the thought of opinionated people.

Reva thought he and Beth were a perfect match. Maura thought they were anything but.

And both women thought they were always right.

Chapter Sixteen

The mid-November sun was bright and cold as Beth walked out of church on Sunday morning, the wind brisk enough to kick up last night's dusting of snow into icy swirls that bit at her ankles.

The usual clusters of folks chatting outside the church dispersed in a flurry of farewells as everyone hurried to their vehicles. Ahead, halfway across the parking lot, Beth saw Elana walking slowly, accommodating Cody's weak leg. She hurried to catch up.

"Can we talk, for just a minute?"

Elana's eyes filled with uncertainty. She turned to shoo Cody into the car, then moved to the back bumper, probably not wanting the boy to overhear them. "Is—is it about this car? If it isn't okay for me to use it, I understand. I will bring it back right away."

"Goodness—of course it's all right. It was just sitting at Sloane House, anyway. On a day like this you wouldn't want to hike a long way to church." Through the back window, she could see Cody putting on headphones attached to a portable CD player. "It's about what you said at our meeting. About you planning to move out."

Elana nervously fingered the keys in her hand. "I... we can make it. It's okay."

"Is this about Roberto? Have you heard from him?"

Elana hunched into her thin coat. "No."

"Someone else?"

"I should be independent. A good example for my son, who will need to stand on his own two feet someday and not be afraid."

"If someone is facing a real threat, there's no shame in being afraid. It's *wise* to take every precaution. If not just for yourself, then for Cody. What would it do to him if he saw you being hurt? Or if he was hurt, and you couldn't protect him?"

Elana bowed her head.

"Promise me that you'll stay at the boardinghouse at least until your classes start. By then, you'll have money in savings, and the money for a down payment on an apartment. You'll know about your financial aid, and not have to worry. And—" Beth took a deep breath. "For Cody's sake, if not your own. At Sloane House you have family—people who care."

Long seconds ticked by before Elana finally lifted her head. "We'll stay."

Checking in on Frank had become the pivotal point in his day, Dev realized as he stepped off the elevator and sauntered down the corridor to the familiar hospital room.

A man who'd started out as a stranger, an unwanted

responsibility, had firmly settled in Dev's heart, like the father he'd always wanted.

Nonjudgmental, undemanding, with his wry wit and piercing assessments, Frank was the kind of guy Dev hoped he would be, if he reached a grandfatherly age.

He certainly didn't want to end up like his temperamental old man.

At Frank's open door, Dev knocked lightly before stepping inside and set a copy of the *Wall Street Journal* on the bedside table. "How are you doing? Ready to take on the world?"

"Better." Though he must have been up for a shower, shave and breakfast earlier, Frank was lying back against the elevated head of the bed with the covers pulled up to his shoulders, and his usual tangle of IV lines snaking up to the fat, clear bags of fluid hanging by his bed.

He looked exhausted, his skin pale and sagging in folds on his face and neck.

Dev settled a hip on the broad windowsill and unzipped his jacket. "So what's happening? Did they make you run a marathon this morning?"

"Physical therapy *and* occupational therapy starting at seven-thirty in the morning," he grumbled, though there was still an irrepressible sparkle in his pale blue eyes. "And the vampire woman came by at four, wanting her daily vial of blood."

Dev laughed. "They just don't want you to enjoy this place too much, so you'll get well and go home."

"They're doing a fine job of it. Thanks for the newspaper, by the way."

"We finally had our first monthly meeting at Sloane House. Everyone wished you were there."

That earned a half smile.

"Let's see….Elana has been accepted at the community college, but hasn't received the news about her financial aid package yet. She's talking about wanting her own place, though."

"Good for her. She's a fine mama to that little boy of hers."

"Beth is going to help Carl work on his long-term disability benefits this week."

"Carl suffers more than a body should. He deserves those benefits, and more."

"Let's see. Who's left…" Dev grinned at him "Reva. I understand a friend wants her to move to Michigan, and her cousin wants her to move to Florida, because they each have businesses she could manage. But the oddest thing…she wants to stay right here in Aspen Creek, so she's starting to look harder for a job. Now, why would she want to do that?"

The sudden tension in Frank's shoulders eased. "I have no idea."

"She's one classy lady, Frank. How long have you two known each other?"

"We haven't. Well, not really. She was married of course, until her husband died last year. I was just a teacher, and never traveled in their social circle. But… I'd always admired her. Lovely woman, so smart."

"That she is."

"I hardly dared talk to her at the boardinghouse. What would she want with an old gray-haired, unemployed schoolteacher? But since the accident, she comes to see me every day and we have long talks." His smile turned rueful. "Guess now I see what I've missed all these years, by not settling down. Companionship is a wonderful thing. Too bad I had to just about kill myself to find that out."

Dev glanced at his watch and stood. "I'd better be going. I'm short a right-hand man at the moment, and I have some shipments coming in."

Frank beckoned to him as he started for the door. "Just one thing."

Dev dutifully returned to Frank's bedside and rested his hands on the upraised side rail.

"A marine and a quiet high school teacher couldn't be further apart, so you probably don't think you and I are much alike. But in some ways, we are. I was a loner—guess I still am, mostly. I'm independent, sort of stubborn. I look back and see a pretty little gal I liked a lot—but I let her slip through my fingers. Maybe I would have had kids and grandkids by now. A real family.

"And then I look at you and Beth, and I see sparks there, but neither of you is paying attention, and you're going to lose out on something good. You're going to end up like me, son, if you're not careful."

The tourist crowds had thinned after the Harvest Festival during the last weekend of October, leaving the town to the locals once more. Come Thanksgiving, the holiday weekenders would start flooding back for the festive Victorian Christmas decorations, overflowing gift shops, and the quaint little restaurants and B and B's tucked into the surrounding hills.

Beth smiled to herself as she stepped outside for a brisk, early-morning walk through town before opening her store for the day.

With Thanksgiving less than a week away, the rhythmic jangling of bells and clopping of Clydesdale hooves would soon be echoing through town on the weekends, as the massive horses pulled brightly painted wagons with bench seats and roofs decorated in twinkling Christmas lights. Aspen Creek's own version of shuttle buses to and from the parking lots out on the perimeter of town had always charmed her, year after year.

She paused in front of the empty sandstone block building next to the bookstore and looked up at the mullioned windows set deep in the casements.

The building had such potential, it never failed to spur little daydreams about how it could become a focal point for the entire community if it ended up in the right hands.

At the sound of footsteps, she saw Dev sauntering down the sidewalk toward her. "Did you go see Frank this morning?

He nodded. "He's doing well, though he's anxious to be released."

"I don't blame him a bit. How long were you in Walter Reed?"

"Too long." He followed her gaze. "All of these buildings along here are so unique. They look like they'll stand for another hundred years."

She smiled at his abrupt, obvious change of topic.

"I'd been saving for a down payment to buy this one, but it wasn't for sale at any rate…and now soon it will be yours. Any idea what you'll want to do with it if we manage to meet the stipulations of your mother's will?"

"I haven't thought that far ahead. I definitely don't want anything on this block torn down." He leaned back to look at the fortresslike roofline. "Why would you want it? To expand your store?"

"I've always been afraid that someone might buy it and turn it into a bar, or just tear it down and put in something new and ugly. It has those wonderful old high, pressed-tin ceilings and hardwood floors, and I suppose it could be a trendy setting for some yuppie bar, but I think the main floor would be lovely as a gift shop and a nice venue for parties, a wedding chapel, or perhaps a photographer's studio. The upstairs would be perfect for a youth center. Our town doesn't have anything like that, and we need a good, safe place around here for the kids."

A bright red BMW pulled up in front of the law offices on the other side of the street. Nora Henderson climbed out, a briefcase in her hand, her trim, black skirt suit and severely combed chignon suggesting that she would be in court today.

She smiled, waved, then looked both ways and crossed the street to join them, her high heels smartly clicking on the asphalt. "I got the report you e-mailed last night. Thanks."

"One month down and five to go," Beth said. "I think things are going pretty well."

"I also got a fax from Stan Murdock."

Dev snorted. "I'm sure he's rubbing his hands in anticipation, waiting for us to fail."

"Oh, he's doing more than that. He has a lawyer going over the will in great detail. I have a feeling he'll demand documentation of exactly how you two are meeting your mother's wishes—but he'll wait until the very end of the six-month period to do so, hoping to catch you when it's too late for you to make corrections."

"I like him less the more I hear," Beth murmured. "He stopped in one day, and said we had no chance of success with Sloane House. He offered me cash to just give up."

"You did say no."

"Of course. I want to help those people, not walk away. Just keeping the place open as long as we can is the biggest help of all. Stan has no claims unless Dev and I fail with the boardinghouse…correct?"

"Absolutely. His lawyer has also talked to me about what he terms the vague, subjective nature of the parameters defining the success of the boarders in the 'real world,' he called it." She shrugged. "I think the man has comprehension problems if he doesn't understand the terms 'gainfully employed' and 'independent living,' but maybe that's just me."

Beth bit her lower lip. "About that…Carl is trying, but he hasn't come up with any employers interested in a guy with chronic health problems. I'll be looking into his disability benefits this week."

"Good. But also try to get him to 'think outside the box,' as it were. I think he'll surprise you."

"And Frank is still in the hospital….but he should be out soon, and we still do have until March."

"You still have that extra six-month extension, but I'd try not to use it if at all possible. Stan is going to pull every string he can, and I'd rather not give him any chance at taking you two down."

"'Taking us down.'" Beth shivered as she and Dev walked to the end of Hawthorne, then headed toward Main. "What an awful term."

"And don't think for a minute that Stan would hesitate to do it. I think he was more interested in the estate than my aunt's death when she passed away. I was just a kid, and even I saw that avaricious gleam in his eyes."

"How sad, if he didn't even love her. A wasted marriage to the wrong man." Her words were barely out before she caught the irony of what she'd said, but Dev didn't seem to notice.

"It happens way too often."

"I always thought your parents seemed happy together." At Dev's dry laugh, she looked up at him. "Well, I know they were a little too busy to be parents, but they seemed to get along well. Not that I mean to pry."

"It's no secret. They were happy enough with each other. Their problem was having a son who didn't conform to expectations, as you well know." The dimple in his left cheek deepened. "I always thought a dozen siblings would have been nice, so I could get lost in the crowd. Maybe I would have even ended up following in Dad's footsteps, if he hadn't harped on it so much."

Their hands brushed as they walked and she veered

away, but he caught her hand and held on for a few strides, then released his hold when they reached Main.

The stores were still closed and the streets were nearly empty, save for the cars nosed to the curb in front of the Dancing Lily tearoom, which offered scones and French pastries during the morning hours.

"Do you have time for coffee?"

She looked up at the old-fashioned clock jutting out over the door to Ray's Barbershop. The hands, shaped like scissors, were always at least twenty minutes fast, so it had to be close to ten. Still, she wavered, before shaking her head. "I need to get back. The Happy Frogs day-care group is coming for a tour, so I need to get ready."

"I bet that'll be wild."

"It is, but I love it. Kids that age are so precious."

She hadn't meant to sound wistful. She usually took care to keep her inner longing well hidden from family and friends, because they'd invariably urge her to date more—as if that would instantly lead to white picket fences, apple pies on the sill and 2.3 perfect kids.

Only her mother and Dev knew the score in that regard. No happily-ever-afters, no stair-step kids with long chestnut curls, all lined up in their Sunday best for church each week.

They continued down the block, past the quilting shops, the high-end galleries, the boutiques with price tags carefully hidden from the stares of passersby.

"So how come you didn't remarry?"

She'd thought he'd missed the tone in her voice, and

she'd just breathed an inner sigh of relief. Now, his question sucker punched her in the midsection.

"I…date. I've met wonderful guys and enjoyed their company, but I like my life as it is. I'm content, aren't you? We both ended up with what we wanted, or we'd be leading totally different lives right now. Totally." She was embarrassed, and she was *babbling* and couldn't seem to stop. "I mean…being single means you can do what you want, when you want, and not answer to anyone."

At his continuing silence as they took a right and the Walker Building came into view, she ventured a quick glance at him. At least he wasn't laughing…or worse, radiating sympathy for the pathetic ex-wife who apparently had no life.

He stopped in front of the building, where a new forest-green sign was leaning against the front. "What do you think of the sign?"

Old-fashioned gilt letters swirled out the name *Sloane Sports*—nearly identical to the style of the sign over at the boardinghouse. "It's beautiful. Great name, too… easy to remember."

He stared down at her, his eyes intent and searching her own. "I really enjoyed walking with you. Maybe another time?"

"Just holler if you see me. I try to get out every day, rain or shine."

He strolled away and she continued on to her store, reining in the temptation to look back.

Just a walk. A casual conversation. Nothing more than she'd do with anyone else in town…yet she could still feel the tingle in the hand he'd held, still felt that little sense of loss when he'd released it.

And there was no use denying it to herself. The old chemistry was still there, at least for her, and it fanned brighter every time she ran into him, no matter how brief and innocuous the meeting. She wouldn't let it go further. But how hard was it going to be with him establishing his business just down the street?

Her heart caught painfully at the thought. What would it be like when he brought a girlfriend back to town someday, or even a wife?

She closed her eyes. Said a little prayer.

Then she hurried on to her meeting with the Happy Frogs, and hoped she'd someday be able to forget her feelings for Devlin Sloane.

Chapter Seventeen

Beth cradled her mug of hot tea with both hands and studied Sophie's worried expression. "You've just got one semester left, right? Surely things will work out."

Sophie fingered the wedding rings she still wore on her right hand. "I hope so…but it's all like a house of cards, just waiting for the first breeze. My financial aid is half what it was last year, and now the restaurant is cutting back its hours over the winter, because business has been slow."

"Maybe you can pick up another job?"

"I'll sure try, but it's tricky, with my long commute and my class schedule. And in the spring we'll have long hours of practicum at the hospital." A corner of her mouth rose in a wry grin. "My life sounds like quite a soap opera, doesn't it?"

"I think you are *amazing*. Just think of what you're doing—raising a son, going to school full-time, supporting yourself. How many people could do what you're doing? Just getting into the physical therapy program was tough. I can't imagine how difficult those classes are. You need a T-shirt with Super Mommy on it."

Sophie broke into laughter. "Stop. You're making me blush."

"Well, it's true. I'm so proud of you. When Rob died, you were so devastated that you didn't know where to turn. And look at you now."

"Well...I just hope I can continue. My parents are talking about moving again. They want to start spending their winters down south, before they're too old to enjoy it...or make it their year-round home. And they *should,* if that's what they want."

"But then you won't have them to watch over Eli."

"It's selfish of me, I know...but Eli can be a handful, and he needs consistency. I'm praying that they'll stay here just one more winter so I can finish college and get a decent job." She bit her lower lip. "They've just been wonderful, letting him stay there on weekends so I can pick up some extra shifts at the restaurant. And after school..."

"No one can care for a child like his grandma," Beth said with a smile.

"Especially one with special needs. And they refuse to let me pay them a nickel, which is a blessing because money has been so tight."

"If they do go, you'll need someone every day after school and on the weekends, right?"

"Not every day. It'll depend on my spring class schedule during the week. And I'm hoping for more regular waitress shifts on Friday and Saturday nights, because the tips are better."

"Do you think he'd be willing to come to the bookstore after school?"

Sophie's eyes widened. "I wasn't hinting. I know you're not in the day-care business. And what single gal wants to spend her Friday and Saturday nights babysitting?"

"The weekdays are no problem. I'm at the store from ten until nine in the evening anyway." Beth took another sip of her peach tea. "He could have supper with me if need be. And the weekends…we could work that out. If you can arrange something else, fine…but otherwise, I can help."

Sophie blinked and sat back in her chair, her eyes wide. "You are the most wonderful, best friend ever. *Ever.* I won't impose on you like that, but the fact that you'd even offer is just incredible."

"It's not imposing. And I'll be disappointed if you don't let him come over on the weekdays at least." Beth grinned. "He's a good kid, and he always behaves well at the store. And hey, since I'm destined to be a childless, crotchety old spinster, I'll consider it a favor if I can enjoy him for a while."

"Thank you," Sophie said fervently. "Maybe my parents will stay in town. But just knowing there's another good option is such a relief." She paused, then her eyes took on a wicked gleam. "But I don't know about this 'crotchety old spinster' stuff. Maybe you and I should try one of those online dating services after I graduate, just to see who is out there. Maybe there's an Adonis with a PhD, just around the corner. A perfect Mr. Right."

Beth smiled, but shook her head. "I had my experience with a Mr. Right—I truly thought he was. But after that, I think I'll just be happier to live alone."

Beth walked into Sloane House and inhaled the wonderful aromas of sage, parsley, butter and onion. Lots and *lots* of melted butter.

"Oh, my word. This is incredible," she breathed. "Someone is making dressing for Thanksgiving tomorrow, and I don't think I can wait until then."

From the settee in the parlor, Frank waved his cane at her and laughed. "Imagine coming home to this today, after almost four weeks in the hospital. Home cooking, and Thanksgiving to boot."

"I'm just thankful for the invitation tomorrow." She walked into the parlor and leaned over to give him a hug, careful to avoid the leg propped up on a footstool and pillows. "Maybe we can raid the kitchen when Elana and Reva aren't looking."

"Maybe." Frank gave her speculative look. "I hear you're bringing pecan and peach pies, and cranberry-orange bread. Is that pecan pie good?"

"My grandma's recipes, all of them. So I don't dare tamper with them." She winked at him as she sat on one of the carved walnut chairs flanking the settee. "I'd be in the doghouse until *next* Thanksgiving if I did." She looked around, curious. "Where is everyone?"

"Carl is puttering on his car. Cody and the women-folk are in the kitchen." Frank raised an eyebrow. "And in case you're interested, Dev brought me home from the hospital and then had to leave right away for a noon appointment at the VA in St. Paul."

"The hospital?"

"Something about a required second checkup. He looked mighty tense about it, too. I think he has a lot riding on a clean bill of health. It's already almost eight o'clock, so he oughta be home be now, wouldn't you think?"

She sank against the back of her chair.

Dev had made no secret of his plans to go back into active service as soon as he'd healed and had satisfied his commitment to Vivian's will. He'd been crushed when his first VA appointment revealed that he no longer qualified for active service. Permanently. So what was this about? If the Marines had some sort of change of heart, would he disappear into the Middle East again for years?

A hollow, aching place in her heart started to grow.

"You could convince him to stick around, you know," Frank mused. "He might find Aspen Creek is the very place he should put down roots."

"I don't think anyone will convince him of that. He'll follow his heart…and I have a feeling it's anywhere but here." She stood and looked out the window toward the cottage, where she could see the glow of a solitary lamp through the living room curtains. "Does he leave lights on when he goes?"

"I've never noticed. If you see a light in there, maybe you should check it out." Frank chuckled. "You can get a start on letting him know why he should stay around."

Grabbing her purse and keys, she headed for the front door. "Great to have you back, Frank. See you tomorrow!"

Darkness had fallen, but silvery moonlight filtered through the thick, bare branches overhead, creating paisley designs of light and shadow on the stone walk. A nervous flutter started dancing in her stomach when she reached up to knock on the door, but the door was ajar, so she gently pushed it with her fingertips. It swung wide with a soft creak.

Bent over at the antique oak desk near the fireplace, Dev jerked upward at the sound and spun around, his face tense and drawn.

"I hear you went to the VA today. How did it go?"

The expression in his eyes grew dark, unreadable. "They wanted a final checkup on my shoulder, and I asked them to reexamine my hearing. There's actually been some improvement in my hearing—something the previous doc said would never happen." A half smile tilted one corner of his mouth. "The shoulder is still weak, but maybe I'll defy the odds. They told me to report to North Carolina. If the docs there agree, I may have another chance for combat duty."

The room seemed to fall away as she processed his words. "What about Sloane House? Your inheritance?"

"I talked to Nora. She said she couldn't in good conscience force a soldier to stay home over this, especially since you live here permanently and the residents have been making such good progress. They've made some really positive comments about both of us, which helped."

"So, y-you're leaving. Just like that."

"It's been my life. I feel…cast adrift. Everyone I know is in the military."

"Not everyone," she said softly. She moved closer and rested a hip against the overstuffed chair by the fireplace, not trusting her knees. After years of trying to forget him, her traitorous heart had fallen for him all over again. "You have people who are like family right here in town. Carl and Reva and Cody." *And me.* "People who care. What about your store? And Frank?"

He rubbed his jaw. "Frank is a natural. He reads up on everything, and is turning into quite an encyclopedia on the sports merchandise we offer. And he's great with the customers. He'll be a wonderful manager whether I'm around or not."

"But…you once said that you never wanted to be behind a desk."

Dev turned and rested his hands on her shoulders and brushed a brief kiss against her forehead. "Apparently that's no longer an issue. On the way to the base I need to do some thinking."

She savored the warmth of his hands and the sweet, electric sensation of his gentle kiss, not wanting to read anything more into the reassuring gesture that it was.

Because soon he'd walk right back out of her life.

Chapter Eighteen

Maura stopped at the entryway of the bookstore, dropped her bags at her feet and swooped close for a hug and a kiss on the cheek. "I'm so glad to be home for Christmas," she said, her bangle bracelets clinking and gauzy scarves shimmering in the glow of the twinkling Christmas lights strung around the interior of the store. "It was wonderful that Olivia had to pick up her daughter at the airport, so she could give me a ride."

"I can't believe you're here." Beth hugged her back. "How long can you stay?"

"Just a few days. But I'm thinking of moving back this coming year, if I can sell the gallery. A health scare can sure affect one's priorities, and losing two assistant managers in the past three months has been the last straw." Maura stepped back and held Beth's shoulders, her eyes shining with tears. "I've missed you, sweetheart."

Long after Maura had gone upstairs to unpack, Beth paced through the bookstore. She'd gone over the day's receipts, feeling lonelier than she had in months.

Even the twinkling icicle lights in the bay window and the pine-scented candle burning on the counter by the cash register didn't lift her mood.

She hadn't seen Dev since just after Thanksgiving, and Frank said that he'd left for Camp Le Jeune a week ago.

Dev hadn't even stopped to say goodbye. Which was just as well, because the warmth in his gaze had faded right after Thanksgiving, and their relationship had faded right along with it.

If she'd begun to imagine anything more from him, she'd been a fool a second time around, and she deserved what she got…though a weight heavy as an anvil pressed down on her chest as she took one last glance around the store and blew out the single fragrant candle, then shoved her cell phone into her coat pocket.

Frank had been opening Sloane Sports each day, though, with the help of two new clerks, and it appeared that the influx of Christmas shoppers coming to Aspen Creek from the surrounding cities had really taken to the new store. With his new full-time job and the one Reva had accepted at a local jewelry store, they were now planning a small Christmas Eve wedding and a move to a small rental house across town, and Beth couldn't remember ever seeing a couple so giddy, so totally in love…made all the sweeter in two people approaching the autumn of their lives.

Carl was finally receiving his disability payments, and he'd started to work part-time at Sloane Sports as well, so he was beginning to think about independent living, too.

And Elana—Beth smiled, thinking about how she'd blossomed at the bookstore during the hectic Christmas rush. The way she'd calmly stood up to several difficult male customers and handled their complaints had been a real turning point in her self-confidence. Cody had been making great strides, too, nurtured under the loving wings of his two foster granddads at the boardinghouse, along with Dev, whenever he was around.

These were the most important people to worry about, and they were now moving into their new lives more quickly than she'd ever expected. So if her own life was a mess, she knew it would just take time to get back on track—and the beautiful candlelight Christmas Eve service next week would surely do the trick.

But now Elana could close up for the night, and it was time to go upstairs. At least with Maura back for a visit, the Christmas decorations and twinkling lights wouldn't seem quite as lonely.

Snow had blanketed the cars on the street, and still swirled under the street lamps like weightless diamonds as she stepped outside the store and fitted her key into the dead bolt of the door leading upstairs.

A shadow fell across the landing and she raised a hand in greeting. "The store is still open—go right on in."

"I'm not here for the books. I've come back for you."

Startled at hearing the deep timbre of his familiar voice, Beth turned and stared at Dev, still not believing that he'd come. "I thought you'd left for good. Y-you didn't even say goodbye."

"I knew I wanted to be here more than anywhere else in the world, so when the VA docs out East offered a medical discharge based on my shoulder injury, I didn't have to think too hard about it."

There'd been a heavy weight around her heart for so many years that she'd come to accept it. But now part of it lifted at his words. "What did you decide?"

"Given my previous injuries and my shoulder, I accepted the medical discharge. I'll be home for good, Beth...if you think you can stand having me around."

She stared up at him in wonderment. "Y-you're going to stay? Here in Aspen Creek?"

He dropped a kiss on her forehead, then a longer one on her lips. "I need to, because I want to spend the rest of my life trying to convince you that we still have a chance together...if you'll let me."

Joy washed through her, along with a feeling of completion that she'd never expected to experience again. "Absolutely."

The door of the store opened, sending golden light across the snowy sidewalk, and Elana and Cody stepped outside.

"Welcome home, Dev," Elana said, her eyes shining. "Welcome home."

Cody giggled. "Are you going to kiss her *again?*"

Dev laughed as he looked down at Beth with a world of love in his eyes. "If I could kiss her every day for the rest of my life, I'd be the happiest man on earth."

* * * * *

Dear Reader,

I hope you've enjoyed your visit to Aspen Creek! This is the first book in the ASPEN CREEK CROSSROADS series, involving the members of a book club in a scenic little Wisconsin town. Though my next book, *Murder at Granite Falls* (April 2011) will be a Love Inspired Suspense title, I can't wait to come back to Aspen Creek after that, for Sophie's story!

Writing for Steeple Hill Books has been a dream come true. I love writing about people like Devlin and Beth, who have encountered challenging times in their lives and find it difficult to let go of the past. Finding a way to forgive, heal and move on can free all of us to enjoy a happy and abundant life...but sometimes it's just so hard to take that step. I have always found such comfort and encouragement in the following Bible verses, and if you are hurting inside, perhaps it will touch your heart, too.

"Don't worry about anything. Instead, pray about everything. Tell God what you need, and thank Him for all He has done. If you do this, you will experience God's peace, which is far more wonderful than the human mind can understand. His peace will guard your hearts and minds as you live in Jesus Christ."
—Philippians 4:6, 7

I love to hear from readers. If you are online, you can reach me at www.roxannerustand.com or through my "All Creatures Great and Small Blog," where authors and readers can exchange stories about their favorite friends with feathers, fin or fur…and horses, too! The blog is at roxannerustand.blogspot.com. You can also e-mail me at www.roxannerustand.yahoo.com. My snail mail address is P.O. Box 2250, Cedar Rapids, Iowa 52403-2550.

Wishing you many blessings,

Roxanne

QUESTIONS FOR DISCUSSION

1. Beth treasures her friendships with the book club members who meet at her store, and considers these women her extended family. Are you geographically close to your family? Far away? What people are you closest to emotionally, and why?

2. Beth worries when she realizes that her ex-husband and her mother are going to be back in town at the same time. Do you have to deal with awkward relationships when certain friends or members of your family are together? How do you think Beth should have handled this situation?

3. What were Devlin's reasons for wanting a divorce? Were they valid? Is divorce ever an appropriate option? Why or why not? Do you think his emotional issues, from what he experienced in the war in the Middle East, played a part in his reactions and decisions when back in the States?

4. Devlin struggles with feeling at ease when back in his hometown. Do you think this is a common reaction for those coming home from the military? Is there a way you could ease the adjustment for someone in your own community?

5. Devlin believes that God has ignored his prayers for years—even his heartfelt prayers during

battle. How does God answer prayers? How has He answered yours? Were you ever surprised by a perfect answer to your prayers—an answer or solution that you hadn't even thought to ask for?

6. Maura has urged Beth to reveal her biggest, most painful secret to Dev. Should Maura just go ahead and tell him? Is it better to keep secrets that may cause someone pain? Does Devlin have a right to know this one?

7. Frank longs to be an active, contributing member of society again, and though he has been a bachelor all of his life, he has strong feelings for Reva. Do you know of older couples who have finally found the love they've always longed for?

8. Elana is frightened and wary, after her past experiences. Does your community have services for abused women like her? How might you help someone who is, or was, in Elana's situation?

9. Several characters in this book are hoping for a fresh start in life, after troubling circumstances waylaid their plans. Are there community colleges or social services in your area that are designed to reeducate and then help people reenter the work force?

10. Vivian was not a loving, attentive mother, but she seems to have become a different person as she

grew older—more giving of her time and more involved in her church. What might have spurred her to change? Can a person ever undo all of their past wrongs? Is there anything that cannot be forgiven? Vivian and Devlin were still estranged at the time of her death. How might she have handled her relationship with Devlin better in the last few years of her life?

11. Book club member Sophie has been widowed for ten months, and is still mourning the loss of her late husband. She notes that some people think she's had plenty of time to move on emotionally. Do you agree? How long does it take to feel "normal" again after the loss of a loved one? What can friends and family do to help? Do you think it's better to bring the subject up, so the person can have a chance to talk about her feelings, or does it just make them feel worse?

12. Devlin returns to town, wanting a second chance at a relationship with Beth, and hoping to readjust to civilian life. What challenges do you think he will face in trying to do so? Since he walked away from Beth once before, do you think she can trust him to stay?

Love Inspired®

TITLES AVAILABLE NEXT MONTH

Available November 30, 2010

REQUEST YOUR FREE BOOKS!

2 FREE INSPIRATIONAL NOVELS
PLUS 2
FREE
MYSTERY GIFTS

Love Inspired

LIREG10R

HARLEQUIN®

A Romance

FOR EVERY MOOD™

Spotlight on
Classic

Quintessential, modern love stories
that are romance at its finest.

See the next page
to enjoy a sneak peek from
the Harlequin® Romance series.

MIA caught sight of Jarrett when he walked into the open lobby. It was hard not to notice the man. In a charcoal business suit with a crisp white shirt and striped tie covered by a dark trench coat, he looked more Wall Street than small-town Colorado.

Mia couldn't blame him for keeping his distance. He was probably tired of taking care of her.

Besides, why would a man like Jarrett McKane be interested in her? Why would he want to take on a woman expecting a baby? Yet he'd done so many things for her. He'd been there when she'd needed him most. How could she not care about a man like that?

Heart pounding in her ears, she walked up behind him. Jarrett turned to face her. "Did you get enough sleep last night?"

"Yes, thanks to you," she said, wondering if he'd thought about their kiss. Her gaze went to his mouth, then she quickly glanced away. "And thank you for not bringing up my meltdown."

Jarrett couldn't stop looking at Mia. Blue was definitely her color, bringing out the richness of her eyes.

"What meltdown?" he said, trying hard to focus on what she was saying. "You were just exhausted from lack of sleep and worried about your baby."

He couldn't help remembering how, during the night, he'd kept going in to watch her sleep. How strange was that? "I hope you got enough rest."

She nodded. "Plenty. And you're a good neighbor for

coming to my rescue."

He tensed. Neighbor? *What neighbor kisses you like I did?* "That's me, just the full-service landlord," he said, trying to keep the sarcasm out of his voice. He started to leave, but she put her hand on his arm.

"Jarrett, what I meant was you went beyond helping me." Her eyes searched his face. "I've asked far too much of you."

"Did you hear me complain?"

She shook her head. "You should. I feel like I've taken advantage."

"Like I said, I haven't minded."

"And I'm grateful for everything…"

Grasping her hand on his arm, Jarrett leaned forward. The memory of last night's kiss had him aching for another. "I didn't do it for your gratitude, Mia."

Gorgeous tycoon Jarrett McKane has never believed in Christmas—but he can't help being drawn to soon-to-be-mom Mia Saunders! Christmases past were spent alone…and now Jarrett may just have a fairy-tale ending for all his Christmases future!

Available December 2010,
only from Harlequin® Romance®.

Love Inspired
HISTORICAL
INSPIRATIONAL HISTORICAL ROMANCE

Beginning January
get *more* of what you love
with **FOUR NEW** engaging stories
rich with romance, adventure and
faith set in a variety of vivid historical
times, available every month from
the Love Inspired® Historical line.

**Also look for our other
Love Inspired® genres, including:**

Love Inspired®

Enjoy six heartwarming and
inspirational romances every month.

Love Inspired®
SUSPENSE
RIVETING INSPIRATIONAL ROMANCE

Enjoy four contemporary tales
of intrigue and romance every month.

ISBN-13:978-0-373-87633-4

Love Inspired®

Home To Heal...
And Reconcile?

When wounded marine Devlin Sloane comes
back to Aspen Creek, he's surprised by his late
mother's will. His new business partner for the
next six months is Beth Carrigan. His ex-wife.
This might prove Dev's most difficult mission yet.
He's never stopped loving the sweet bookstore
owner, but his military career broke them apart.
Now, as Beth and Dev work together helping
others get a new start on life, Dev hopes that he
can break down the walls between them.
And explore the possibilities of a new life
and love together.

Aspen Creek Crossroads:
Where faith, love and healing meet

$5.50 U.S./$6.50 CAN.

ISBN-13:978-0-373-87633-4

50550

9 780373 876334

Steeple
Hill®

INSPIRATIONAL
Love Inspired®
www.SteepleHill.com